THE HUNT

L.R. HICKS

LeeLoo Publishing / Texas

LeeLoo Publishing™
http://leeloopub.com/

First Print Edition

ISBN: 978-0-9988843-4-9
Library of Congress Control Number: 2019941071

ALSO BY L.R. HICKS

Samiyah

CONTENTS

ACKNOWLEDGMENTS

Lady Vi and Wuffle Puff, you came through for me again! I can't thank you enough my darlings. I also want to thank my editor and cover artist, Anne Coffer, and the team at LeeLoo Publishing for their support.

BEFORE THE HUNT

I hate the Hunt. It's foolish. Old fashioned. Archaic. Barbaric.

Every five years a new Hunt begins. Unclaimed women between the ages of fifteen to twenty are thrown out into the wilderness of our island to fend for themselves while the men of the tribe track them down and claim them as their own. I'm on the older end of the scale; twenty. I missed the last hunt, by a hair, and hope to pass this one by as well, but Jamir comes to the hut this afternoon to tell me my fate. The old man leers as he passes the news to my older sister. Her third baby bounces on her hip as she watches him disappear down the trail to the village.

We live on the outermost edge. The farthest away from the populace we can be and remain safe from raids and weather. At night the village torches glow against the dilapidated walls of our hut, but we are alone. Not outcast, but not welcome. No social circles lay in want of our company. Our parents died when we crawled. My sister takes care of me. And I her. My niece and nephews are the result of her now deceased hutmate, Pandin. He wasn't good for her. To her. To me. Or the children. When he died to the waves of a storm off the coast of our island six moonspins ago, neither of us were sad to see him go. Neither was the village, but the food he provided and items he got us…I miss those. He found my sister in her Hunt five years ago. A Hunt I almost had to participate in.

After Pandin told me he intended to hunt for me when the time came, I prayed to the Seer every night for his death. When I got my wish, I regretted it for a whole minute. My sister's happier now without him. We all are. We're just a little hungry.

The little runts run around our hut, playing and laughing as I glare at Jamir's old frame disappearing down the trail to the village.

"That lecher would hunt for you if he could," my sister mutters, sticking her breast into her baby's mouth. Mirana, my sister, doesn't help me any when it comes to the Hunt. She's fertile, having birthed three children in almost five spins around the sun. Though I lack her exotic beauty, I'm still in danger.

I take in a lungful of air, "I know."

"Eighteen days," she repeats his message. "Then what? I'm left alone. That's what." She hunches down to pass through the open doorway of our hut.

I follow her into the small crumbling structure of mud and bamboo with a palm thatch roof. Though lazy, Pandin hunted all right. He kept our bellies full and our skin warm in the wet season. He made repairs to the hut when absolutely necessary. I suppose that's what matters, but his motivation for taking care of me when he didn't need to became clear when he declared his intention to claim me too. Alluding for me to share his bed with my sister. The pig. He deserved to die. I have no regrets. The Seer sent him where he belongs.

I gag a bit as the memory slinks to the surface. I don't want to end up like Mirana. I might not get so lucky. The Seer might not answer my prayers twice. I run through a mental roster of all those eligible to participate in the Hunt this year.

The first hunter who comes to mind is Kaidin. Of course.

"That's assuming I get caught," I crouch down to pull a basket of fish from the hole in the ground keeping them fresh and cool. The village law forbids a woman like me from hunting, but fishing and gathering is allowed. I can only earn my place as a hunter if I last a whole year in the Hunt. Which doesn't happen. Hunts barely last more than a week, but there have been exceptions. I'll be one of those.

Mirana snorts and shakes her head, detaching her baby and laying him on a worn deerskin blanket in the middle of the floor.

It's still morning and I have work to do. I grab a fish and bite into the meat of it, chewing while I replace the basket and grab an empty one I just made of dried palm leaves.

"Going to shore," I exit the hut.

Mirana grunts and focuses on feeding her children.

Ocean wind blows as I make my way from our hut down to the beach. I inhale. The sky is clear and the sun shines down coating me in warmth as I set down my basket on the sand to braid back my long black hair. I rub my hands over my arms when a chill rolls off the choppy water. I pick up the basket and approach jagged rocks, sucking in my breath as I wade thigh deep. Water slaps against the hard surface of the boulder as I reach out for a handful of mussels. Since Pandin died it's been up to me to provide food. Our skins are thin and weak with age and use. What good skins we can trade for go to the children. I can catch fish, when the Seer is kind to my fishing line, and Pandin's old aunt brings us leftover meat from her own grandsons out of pity.

But I hate pity.

Laughter carries over crashing waves. I pause, my fingers raw, my basket a quarter full, and watch a group of young hunters come into view with their spears in hand. Two of them carry baskets full of meat and treated hides. My mouth waters thinking of all that food. I duck out of sight, pressing against the rock, and will myself to disappear into it.

"Lendhi," I balk, hearing my name over the ocean waves. I can't catch anything else they say, closing my eyes, gripping the basket as cold waves splash over my legs. My deerskins soak.

I'm neither particularly pretty or ugly, but I suppose I do all right. My family line attracts people. They were like this with my sister, my mother, and Mirana tells me even our grandmother. They want our childbearing hips and ample breasts. My family makes good on having babies. And if I didn't love those runts so much, I would hate Mirana for proving them right.

I lean over as the hunters disappear down the shore with their prizes. I return to my business of gathering mussels, clearing the rock of any sustenance I can get my claws on before moving down the shore in the opposite direction of the hunters. I find a few crabs and sea slugs. I quirk my lips. I hate sea slugs, but they're better than nothing. I study the meager contents of the basket and allow myself a moment, just a moment, to fantasize about being caught in the Hunt. If I was caught by the right man...

I shake my head. No. There's no guarantee any hunter who took me would provide for my sister and her runts. I can't risk it. They're all I have. I'm all they have.

It's too late for Mirana to become a hunter herself. This honor is only to those women who remain unclaimed. Mirana was claimed, bore children, and village law says she cannot ever become a hunter. But it's not too late for me.

Heading back to our hut, balancing the basket on my hip, I think about what to expect. We'll gather in the village square where the elders and Vikra, our Perst, or the Seer's representative on earth, will give us their blessings in a ceremony. They'll bring out the shiny bone, a token left to us by our ancestors before the old ones walked after death, and we'll get to oooh and ahhh appropriately before they sends us out into the wilderness. A hunter of any age can track us if he likes, but they have to do more than that. They have to bring us back, physically. So that leaves out those who are out of shape and old, but there are exceptions. Some women lay themselves down on the outer edge of the village to be drug back so they can be hutmates to the old men of the village. The old men whose sons provide their food and shelter. When that old man dies, the sons still have to care for her. If he has no sons, then his daughter's hutmate. Rotten. The lazy hunters who want an easy lay take them up on it. The woman gets her meals, and the hunter gets his woman.

Not me. That's not what I want, but that's not what Mirana wanted either. It's not what most of us want. I will fight until the bitter end. If I can last a year in the wilderness I can become a hunter myself. No hutmate necessary. I'll get us real food and deerskins for the family. Maybe even sealskins. Women before me have done it. Not in some time. Not in my lifetime, but it's happened. I want to be one of those. I need to figure out how.

My thoughts wander back to Kaidin. He's one of the best hunters in the tribe. Best fighters. Best everything. We were friends growing up together in Banki's hut, the place for orphans and cast off hutmates. A place Mirana and I might end up in again if I don't take this seriously. As Kaidin grew in social stature and I shrank from village life, we stopped talking. It just…happened. What I know of him is kindness. To me, at least. Which is all I really care about. I bite my lip, stopping at the stream of fresh water running near the village, kneeling, thinking. Careful not to cut my fingers, I wash off the mussels and other goodies I found for dinner. Yech, sea slugs.

A branch snaps to my left and I shoot to my feet, watching the rustling brush as Jokinah and her father emerge from the foliage with spears in hand. I wave a greeting and they return it, no words necessary. Her father kneels next to the stream and she follows. They drink. Now, *she* is the most beautiful girl in the village. Another favorite of the hunters. It's tradition for her father to teach her survival in the wild. In hopes she can hold out for a good hunter, or in hopes she can hold out all year. Fathers hate their daughters being part of the Hunt, but sure do love it when they're hunting the daughters of others. Jokinah's own father has three hutmates.

I sigh and kneel, getting back to washing. There's no one around to teach me. And Pandin wouldn't have bothered, even if he was here.

I finish my task and return to our hut. The runts sleep while my sister weaves one of her infamous baskets. Much as I do to keep food in our bellies, Mirana works hard for us to have things to trade at market. She's done this for years, and when Pandin caught her she had to stop. In the six months since his death, she's picked it back up like she never left off. She treats the thin slices of bamboo before dyeing them with berries and weaving them into intricate patterns for baskets. They tie together with rolled dyed palm leaves and are both sturdy and beautiful. I sell them for trade at the market. Other villagers are happy to trade for them and with the set she's working on we hope to get some new deerskins for ourselves.

"Hey," I drop the basket and sit next to her, twisting a palm leaf tight. "I have an idea."

"Uh oh," she smiles, not looking up from her weaving.

I thunk her thick thigh. She sucks in her

breath and slaps my bare shoulder. I laugh and fall over.

"What's your idea?" she sifts through an assortment of blue pieces, searching for a matching color.

"I'm going to ask Kaidin to help me."

She draws her dark eyes up to mine and cocks her brow, "Kaidin?"

I nod, smiling. "Yep."

"What makes you think he'll give you the time of day?"

"Well," I wring out the bottom of my split skirt made of old deerskins. Remnant water from the stream drips onto my bare feet. "That's where you come in."

"Now I'm really worried," she chuckles, sliding a new thin bamboo shaving into the pattern. "What do you want?"

"I thought I might offer him a set of your baskets for the time."

She scoffs, "You have any idea how long this takes me?"

"Well, yeah." I line up the shavings for her by shade, "So he'll know what a good trade it is."

She shakes her head.

I continue, "This can keep me here. With you."

Mirana pauses to put her arm around my shoulders. We sit in silence, our eyes on the bright colored leaves she took care to dye and dry out.

A small figure emerges from the darkness of our hut, rubbing her eyes.

"Mama," she says.

I stay my sister with my hand, "I'll get her.

You make baskets!"

Her laugh follows me as I scoop her child into my arms.

It's rare to find Kaidin alone, so at the end of the day, when the sun kisses the horizon, I wait on the empty shore.

When we were children he came out to this stretch of beach to pay respects to his mother. She perished with mine on the same day. During the same raid. I should be a good daughter and do the same, but I can't even remember my parents. He remembers his mother and never knew his father. Though we grew up in Banki's hut together, the tragedy of being orphaned at the same time is our only other connection. As a boy he was valued and taken in as an apprentice hunter. My sister and I were left behind with all the other girls.

My woven basket is half full of small fish I caught in the stream running out into the ocean. I sit on one of the smooth boulders with the incoming tide splashing around me. I set down the basket beside me and curl my legs up to my chest and hug them, watching the sun sink down into the waves. I don't know why, but today I braided my hair back, tight, from my face.

"It makes you look like a seal," Mirana always laughs at me.

It's out of my face and...who cares how I look? I'm not here to entice him. Well, with beauty anyway.

On cue he comes down the village path. His shoulders are broad and his skin is always a shade darker than mine, no matter how long I've spent in the sun. His black hair is tied back with a strip of hide and the dark paint hunters wear in the shape of a handprint covers most of his face. His bare muscular torso is equally decorated in painted handprints and writ-speak, but they're smudged from sweat and a day's hunting. No doubt. Sealskin hangs down from his waist in a wrap; beautiful, in perfect condition and I have to bite down my jealousy as I watch him. I'm so tired of fish meat, mussels, and leftovers. And sea slugs.

His blue eyes glance up to me and he smirks. Heat rushes to my face.

This isn't the first time we meet on the shore, but it's the first in a while.

Instead of sauntering down to his mother's small shrine carved into a boulder, he approaches the edge of the water close to me.

"Lendhi," his baritone carries over the waves. "What are you doing here?"

I grab my basket and jump down, splashing into the cool water. The dying rays of sunlight shine on his skin, coating him in gold. He towers over me now, a spear strapped to his back and a knife hanging from his belt, and he looks down at me, cupping his hand over his brow against the sunlight.

"I have a proposition for you," I pause as he crosses his arms over his chest. "Teach me to hide."

He cocks his dark brow, "You don't talk to me for how many spins around the sun and you want to ask this of me?"

I poke his chest, "*You*, stopped talking to *me*. I

embarrass you."

"That's not true," he gently takes hold of my wrist to flick it down. "*You*, stopped talking to, *me*."

"It doesn't matter who stopped talking to whom. I know we're not friends anymore, but the Hunt is coming."

"Yes," he keeps his expression neutral. I at least know him well enough to know it's forced. "I'm aware."

My grip on the basket tightens, "Are you participating?"

"Of course," he shifts and turns his back to me, walking out of the water to the warm dry sand.

I follow him, "You're the best hunter in the village."

He shrugs, but even he must know it's true, "Renhin might argue that."

I balk. Renhin. He's handsome. And a great hunter, but cold. Mean. I've never heard a good thing about the man. Though my interactions with him are limited at best. Thank the Seer.

"Never mind him," I say. "I need you to teach me how to hunt."

Kaidin's brows raise, "You can't participate on the hunting side."

"I *know*," I set down my basket, rolling my eyes. "That's not what I mean. If you teach me how to hunt I can know how to hide. Not get caught."

He rubs his smooth jaw, "I'll have to teach you how to fight too. It's not just hiding you know."

"I know," I scowl. "In exchange I'll give you a set of my sister's baskets. A hutmating gift. I'm sure Jokinah will love it."

His jaw ticks. I want to cower from the scowl

flashing across his face, but stand my ground. He's the best hunter and she the best catch. It doesn't take calculation and logic to know she's his goal.

"That's a fair trade," his eyes drop to the contents of my basket. I flush under his scrutiny, pulling it behind my hip. His eyes linger, "When do you want to start?"

I wait for Kaidin by the stream at sunrise. My stomach turns in knots. There are no village laws, that I'm aware of, saying we can't do this. It's tradition for my father to teach me these things, but what if I don't have one?

Kaidin strolls into view carrying a smaller spear in addition to the one strapped on his back. I stand and offer him the smallest of my sister's baskets. He takes it, unwraps the worn deerskin I took great care to wash last night, and peeks inside. I packed salted fish for us and he smiles. He reties the wrapping and returns the basket.

"All right," he says, leading me upstream past the village. "Your first concern is hydration."

I nod.

"Thirst will kill you before hunger. It's a rule of three. Remember, three minutes without air, three hours without shelter, three days without water, and three weeks without food."

I nod again. Rule of three. Got it.

"You seem to do okay gathering," he glances at the basket I carry. "And fishing. So today I'm going to work on fresh water. You get yours from the stream here, right?"

"Yes," I dip my toes into the cool running water when we pause.

"There's another one like this by Anaki's Cove." He kneels down and cups his hand to bring water to his lips.

My brows furrow, "On the north side of the island?"

"Yeah," he stands. "I think that'll be your best bet to hide. The mountains shield from the worst of winds and the waters are calmer for better fishing. There're many streams feeding out from those mountains into the cove."

"But it's so far," I bite my lip. "Quite a trek."

"I know," he offers me the smaller spear. "Almost a week. At a brutal pace."

I fill my lungs with air and breathe out slow.

"But most hunters won't go that far. Or even think to look that far north. Most of the women in past Hunts stayed in the immediate area."

"True," I take the spear. Not all women who try to outlast the Hunt survive. It's rare for anyone to venture far from the village, just in case. "But that doesn't mean they won't look."

He nods, "You can always go to Cadmin's Cave or even Spirin's Rest."

"No," I shake my head. "I think you're right about the cove."

We follow the stream into the thicket, where he pushes past foliage, snapping young twigs of bushes and saplings.

"See this?" he points to the broken branches. "Avoid this. Easy way to find someone's path."

I make a mental note.

"If you reach an area like this, take to the trees if you can, or beneath the bush. But if you must go through them, go gently. Don't break the branches. Or cut them, that's even worse."

We push through and I listen as he tells me how to keep my tracks covered.

We spend the day practicing. I hide, taking his advice into consideration, and he hunts for me. He always finds me. Quickly. The bastard. He explains how he did and next time I don't make the same mistake. By the end of the day we double the amount of time it takes him to find me.

The sun sets as I hide on the large branch of a sprawling cover tree. A tree that stands out as foreign against the backdrop of palms and bamboo. Flowers bloom in bright colors and I lay dark and hidden in the thick leaves. Kaidin breaks cover from the thicket and searches. I hold my breath. I took care to approach from the side covered in moss, but this is what gives me away. He traces his fingers over the mussed moss and kneels at the base of the tree before looking up, right to me.

"Ah," he says. "Got ya."

I growl and swing down, hanging from the branch before dropping to my feet.

"You're getting better," he smiles. "I think we're done. I need to go cook some dinner."

"Me too. Those sea slugs aren't going to catch themselves." I smile, then grimace, "Sorry I kept you so long."

He waves it off as we head back towards the village, "It's fine."

We walk in comfortable silence until we reach the stream. I return his spear and offer the basket empty of salted fish.

He slides the small spear into a strap at his back with ease.

"How long does it take your sister to make these?" he examines the basket. "They're beautiful."

I straighten, "Sometimes days. She works hard to get the dye colors perfect before she even starts. They're very durable too, see?" I tug on the edge.

"I do," his hand drops to his side, holding the basket. "You're right. My hutmate will like it. It's not a fair trade though."

My heart skips a beat as I frown, "But—"

"I should do more for you. Doesn't seem fair I spend one day to earn a basket that takes many."

Not what I expect. I'm not foolish enough to contradict him.

"I have an idea," he continues. "If you know for a fact you'll go to Anaki's Cove, I can leave you caches of supplies along the way. I'll put food and water in them for you. Some other things. You'll have to memorize the path I give you though."

My jaw drops, "Really?" I narrow my eyes, "In exchange for what? Can't just be baskets."

"Well, you can send Jokinah my way if you see her," he shrugs. "Help me get her."

I smirk and roll my eyes. He laughs and we continue.

"I don't know how I feel about sabotaging someone else for my gain," I say. "I don't want to condemn her anymore than myself."

He gives me a sidelong glance, "You think giving her to me is condemnation? What makes you think I'll make such a terrible hutmate?"

I quirk my lips.

"Blessed Seer Lendhi," he mutters. "You don't have to think that hard on it."

I laugh.

"So you want to last the year?" he asks.

I nod, "I do."

"Be like old Banki and raise other people's runts?"

He doesn't, thankfully, mention the other women of Banki's hut. If he does I'll slap him.

"Sure," I shrug. "I already raise my sister's. What's a few more?"

"You are good with them," he says.

"But the point, is to be free and do what I want. And to stay with Mirana."

He nods and we stop at the edge of the village. I don't want him to see our hut anymore than he has to. It's embarrassing. Our one room hut stands in disrepair. The thatch roof has holes. The eastern wall sags, creating a gap between the thatch and frame. There isn't a proper wooden door, but a worn deerskin tied at the sides. There's no hole for the fire to exit our ceiling, so we have to open the doorway up, even in the wet months, for smoke to escape. Smoke over time has discolored the mud over the doorframe. There aren't even any windows. I do my best but, with trying to learn to hunt, and gather, and sell my sister's baskets at market…

"You do all this for her?" he asks.

"Yes," I don't hesitate. "And her runts. We're family. And what will happen to her if I'm caught?"

"Your hutmate will provide for them surely," his dark brows furrow.

"That's not a guarantee. I can't count on that."

16

"Pandin took you in," he points down the way where our hut lies.

Heat flushes my cheeks.

"With the intention of making me his second hutmate," I cross my arms.

He screws up his face, eliciting laughter from me.

"My thoughts exactly," I breathe in huffs.

"What if a hunter promises to take them in?" he asks.

I consider him a moment, "I'll give it consideration, but I doubt a civil conversation will happen if I get caught."

This time he laughs, "True. Blessed Seer you have a dirty mouth sometimes."

"Kai," I say, finding myself on familiar ground with him again. All it took was a day. "Do you mean it? You'll really help me? In exchange for sending Jokinah your way?"

He sobers, "I do. I'll do everything in my power to keep other hunters away from you."

"Then you've got a deal," I hold out my hand.

Two weeks until the Hunt.

Kaidin shows me what to do and shares his bounty with me when he goes hunting proper. It's nice. While teaching me how to take down an animal and process it, he gives me half the take. The Hunt is the only time it's acceptable for a woman to do things like this, so we keep it a secret between us. This part he doesn't have to do, but it's nice. He's nice. It almost makes me want his interest to be in me. Almost.

Kaidin shows me all he can in the time we have, but now he leaves to hide supply caches along the path for me. No one's suspicious because it isn't rare for a hunter to leave the village for a week or two to try hunting in less populated parts of the island. We have a plan. I, have a plan. My chest swells with pride, excitement, and crippling fear as the Hunt looms over the horizon. I will last the year. I try not to think about the fact that most Hunts last barely more than a week. Or that Banki, the ancient old goat, is the last woman to earn her freedom. Others have tried. And they are caught, or they die in the wilderness. But not me. Not. Me.

Sometimes, when I see Jokinah, guilt washes over me, but Kaidin's right. He'll be a good hutmate. I think. She'll be fine.

I tighten the sharp head of my new spear with a small rope of hide Kaidin gave me as Mirana walks out of our hut with her oldest runt in hand. If anyone asks, my spear is for fishing only.

"You should have done this sooner," she says, twirling in her new deerskin. A gift from Kaidin. She dips her hip in a mock dance with a smile and wink as I laugh.

"I know," I tie off the thin strip of hide, securing the bone spearhead to the pole. She watches me as I work. For the first time in ages, even before Pandin died, our food baskets are full. We have new skins to ward off the rain. And the rains come soon. Without me here to help, Mirana faces a hard time juggling the runts and food once our stores run out. A year is a long time. A whole spin around the sun.

I tug the spearhead to check its fastening as a shadow blocks my light. Mirana freezes, gripping her daughter's small hand.

My eyes drag up, over muscular legs, a pristine seal skin hanging between them, past hard abs and lean torso, to Renhin. He kneels on one knee before me and my eyes widen as he reaches out to stroke my cheek. I refuse to flinch. Time in the sun bleaches his hair golden and his eyes are blue like ocean waves. Black paint runs down his muscular torso from humidity. I snatch his wrist and flick it away.

He laughs, "Lendhi."

My brows furrow. I never talk to Renhin. In fact, no one does. A boulder settles in my stomach.

"Do you want to trade for baskets?" I ask. I think he bought one once. For his mother. Years ago.

"No. I've come for you," he stands up to his impressive height. He's even taller than Kai. "I'm going to find you and make you mine."

I can't help but smile though sweat runs down my back, "Good luck then."

"I don't need it," he nods to my sister, turning to walk down the trail towards the village.

I let out a held breath and exchange a glance with Mirana.

Seer help me. I don't understand it, but please, Seer, help me.

The Hunt starts tomorrow.

Kaidin got back last night, but I don't talk to him. People watch me now, as they do all the catches.

My sister and I sit in our hut with a fire burning in the pit. On nights like this the ocean wind blows a chill towards the village and I huddle with my nephew under one of the new skins from a deer I helped Kaidin take down.

Mirana sighs, tears pooling in her eyes as she stokes the fire.

"You know what I hate the most?" She doesn't wait for my response, "This is completely out of our control. There's nothing we can do about it."

"Well," I clear my throat, having not spoken in hours. "We can run away, but they'll find us. Then the whole village will hunt us and not just one or two men. And we'll be auctioned at market like your baskets."

"We can make a break for a neighboring island," her dark eyes watch me brush hair back from my nephew's forehead.

"If we were going to do that we should have planned earlier than this," I sigh. "And they have similar customs. And depending on which one we end up at, we can be much worse off. At least here we have…some rights."

"I don't know," she pokes the fire again. Stabbing at the collapsing wood. "Are you sure you don't want to take more food with you?"

I shake my head, "No. I'm leaving it all for you and the kids. I can do this. Live off the land."

In the bylaws of our village, each catch can carry a single bag of items into the wilderness, but they limit the contents of the bag. Mine is small with a full water skin and an extra deerskin blanket that doubles as a cloak with flint and salted fish in addition to deerskins fitted for my feet, at Kai's insistence. We aren't allowed anything like weapons or tents made of hide. No doubt to make it harder, but I'll be fine. The less my burden the faster I can reach Anaki's Cove.

Mirana smiles past the fire between us. Smoke rises to the soot darkened ceiling and crawls along until it escapes out our open door.

THE HUNT

Day One

The Hunt is here.

We stand in the village center before dawn. The glow of sunrise makes the promise of a new day on the horizon hidden by the tree line. Our ages range from fifteen to twenty spins around the sun. Or years in old speech. I stifle a yawn and shift the pack from shoulder to shoulder. We wait on the elders and Perst to give us their blessings before we head off into the wilderness. I glance at Kaidin standing with the other hunters, his arms crossed. I drag my eyes away when he meets my gaze. Mirana isn't here. She stayed back with her runts at the hut, all lined up and waving bye to me with sleepy faces. It was hard to leave them.

My cheeks burn under Renhin's unapologetic stare. I avert my eyes to the sand at my bare feet. Why does he look at me like that? What does it mean?

I swallow and look anywhere but north. Any

hunter watching might catch my intentions if I focus on the direction I plan to travel in. I recite the trail many times in my head. The landmarks and other telltale signs of the caches Kaidin left for me.

My eyes roll as I study those women who don't have packs at all. They're who plan to lay down on the ground for easy capture. In the past, as a child, it was fun to watch. Especially when hunters fought over the most beautiful of the lazy. If more than one hunter wants you they have to fight until either one gives up or one of them is dead. There hasn't been a Hunt death between warriors in many spins around the sun. It's usually not worth it, but there have been a few catch deaths. The hunted. Catches. Us. It's usually exposure. Dehydration. But, some have been murdered by a hunter when resisting capture. Those hunters were punished. Public castration. Murdering a catch is no joke either.

I clasp my hands and squeeze as I think of the many ways I can perish in the next year. If I can last a few weeks I'll be golden. Hunters can't neglect their duties to the village for too long. As far as I know only Renhin is interested enough in me to search longer. I drag my gaze back to him. His light eyes haven't left me. Biting the inside of my lip my focus centers on the elder hut. A flickering glow lights up windows of the longhouse where our village leaders live. Right as the sun peeks over the horizon, creating a harsh canopy of color and shadow past the tree line over the village, the elders and Perst emerge, taking their time, each carrying a different component for our blessing. Some oil from a seal, crushed petals of blue flowers, and antlers of an island deer. Two helpers carry a small decorated bamboo chest behind the Perst. It contains the shiny bone piece.

Layered in deer hides all year, even in the worst heat, their frail bodies are mounds of human buried beneath carcass as they shuffle to us.

They go down the line we form. First, an elder man dips his fingers into the carved wooden bowl of seal oil and smears it across our foreheads. The woman with the crushed petals slides the powder over the line of oil so it sticks to our skin. The last elder, an old man, draws the symbol of the Seer in the paste. An eye with three lines pointing down from the bottom lid. The Perst's job is most sacred, as the chest opens and her shaking hands disappear into it before lifting the shiny bone. The children, those who can't remember the last hunt, gasp as the sun reflects on its surface.

Vikra smiles as she holds the piece, waving it around the first in line's face saying her muttered blessing from the Seer. My heart pounds when they reach me. I look down to my feet and tighten my hands. I flinch when Yanadin's warm thumb wipes oil over my forehead, followed by petal powder, and scratch of the antler. I'm happy it doesn't break my skin and I blink rapidly as a drop of oil slides down past my eye to my nostril. I can't move to wipe it off until I'm long gone. Perst waves the piece I'll never be important enough to touch around my face and circling over my flat stomach. I don't catch all of what she says, no one ever does, but I'm sure it's something to do with fertility and duty and all that nonsense.

The sun shines on us as the elders recite an old prayer, led by the Perst, and Yanadin raises his hand, as though we talk in this silence.

"Catches have until noon," he says. "And then hunters may go find them. No killing the catches, and ladies, no killing hunters. You can fight each other, but no death. Only a death between hunters can be."

I refrain from rolling my eyes. We know this already.

"Go," he says.

I hesitate, as do the others, but turn and run into the tree line. Breaking the spell with movement, others follow me. Hunters whoop and holler after us as we disappear from their view.

I recite the plan I made with Kaidin as I run. First day, get as far as I can as fast as I can. I can't ration my water and will drink it as needed. Walk all night. I'll sleep during the second day since that's the time hunters will look for us. I'm less likely to be spotted if I'm still.

I leave an obvious path, and other catches stumble around me in the brush. Well, those that don't lay down. I reach the stream, wiping the oil and powder from my forehead, and turn around to walk upriver. The village lies north and I pass near, hesitating to hide behind a thick patch of foliage along the stream to watch the activity. In the early morning most of the village goes about to see to their responsibilities. Children run around to play. The elders and Perst are surely gone back to bed, and the hunters stand in groups. Talking. About us. But they're not hunting. Not yet.

They're forbidden to catch us now. They have to let us pass.

I pass the village and head north. Again I recite the landmarks. Follow the stream north until

Deer Cave. Sleep there tomorrow morning. Follow the tree line along the edge of the plains until the Hollowed Tree. I can take shelter in its haunted trunk. After, a long trek to Anaki's Cove, through rainforest and past the plains. Once at the cove I'll be fine and so far gone no one will think to find me there.

I bite my lower lip, smiling. Past the village I run along the shallow stream, water erasing any trace of my path. A snapping twig catches my attention to the left and I halt, toes curling over the smooth rocks of riverbed.

A gasp catches in my throat when Renhin steps from the thicket and leans against the ancient trunk of a palm, snapping a twig into tiny pieces. His light eyes focus on mine. His gaze heats. Behind his calm demeanor muscles tighten, ready for action. He drops the remnants of twig and keeps eye contact as I restart my walk. I hate that he sees the direction I head, but don't worry.

"Lendhi," he says.

I lift my hand. His eyes follow me as I pass, "You can't take me."

"I know," his penetrating gaze keeps my attention. "Not yet."

I narrow my eyes and make a show of turning my back to him, following the stream. In my mind scenarios play out. I can continue this path and hope he doesn't catch on or make a point of turning and head south. Turning around might be more obvious. I press on. His stare follows me past the curvature of the stream. When I'm certain he's no longer in view, I glance back over my shoulder, letting out a held breath. This will work. It has to.

First day isn't a challenge.

I have a full belly and plenty of water. Hunters are out on the trail, but as the sun dips behind the mountains of the Seer, I know I have gone far. Hopefully far enough. Kai instilled in me during our training distance is most important in the first days. I can zigzag through the trees all day long, but in the end, there is always a straight path to me. There is no shortcut for distance.

I slow my pace with the darkness. Weary, tired, I know to be safe I must tread with care through the thicket. I'm not the only predator out here. I cannot possibly hope to travel with a torch to ward off the big cats, as I normally would, for fear of being seen.

The night is long. My feet and hips ache. My water skin's light. I have a handful of salted fish and berries left. I want to stop, but can't. Images of a nameless, faceless hunter pushing me down to have his way with me fuels my legs. I keep going. And finally, sunrise.

But I don't see Deer Cave. I frown. I'm still in the forest. I should be on the edge of the plains by now.

Panic grows with my heartbeat, mimicking the drums of our village dances.

Bone weary, I manage to climb up the rough bark of a palm tree to catch a glimpse of sunrise. I'm facing north. I'm going the right way. I bite my lip, knowing I didn't cover as much distance as I thought last night. Sliding down the tree trunk, I shake off night's cold and wrap my deerskin cloak tighter around my shoulders. I trek on.

When I break the tree line to the plains making up the center of our island, Deer Cave sticks up from the flat land. Not a true cave, Deer Cave was once a settlement of our ancestors, built of mud into a dome. Here they found the shiny bone piece the Perst keeps in her care. Over time a wall collapsed in the dome, making it as a cave. Deer favor its shelter in the wet months and so Deer Cave is the name that sticks. No matter that predators keep clear of it. Or the rumors old spirits haunt the fields around it.

I quirk my lips. I don't believe in spirits. I believe in sleep. In the Hunt. Hunger. Thirst. I approach at a cautious pace.

No animals, predator or prey, inhabit the large structure as I approach. Wind blows warmth from the plains with sunrise. As the great disc rises over the horizon I walk into the shadows of the dome. Untouched trinkets of yesteryear lay about. Yellow grass grows over the remains of softened ancient furniture made of the same mud. I search for subtle signs of disturbance, following broken grass and overturned dirt to the back. Disturbed earth with a new, solid spear propped up against the wall marks my find.

I smile.

My first stash left by Kai. I glance over my shoulder before squatting to dig with my bare hands. I find a deerskin sack, brushing off a layer of dirt, and open it. I hug it to me a moment before widening the opening and sifting through the contents. Fresh, soft, beautiful sealskins. Warm and thick. A full water skin and salted fish. Almost more than I can carry. I eat and drink greedily. Readjusting my supplies, I lay out over the sealskin cloak he wrapped the cache in. Soft and warm, sleep finds me faster than it has in many spins around the sun.

Day Two

For a moment I dream as large hands smooth down the sides of my waist and hips, but as my eyes flutter open a hunter's shadow looms over me with the afternoon sun at his back.

Yondin.

I don't know him well, but his leering smile jolts me from dreamland and my palm snaps out against his jaw. He staggers back as I jump to my feet, grabbing the new spear. I lunge forward, the blunt end toward him, and it collides with his hard stomach. He cries out, falling to his knees, and I scramble to gather my things. He coughs and crawls, reaching out as I scurry past him through the dome and out onto the plains.

I run to the cover of the tree line, following it along the edge of the plains. This is my predetermined path, but he lost sight of me past the trees too. My heart hammers in my chest. Air fills and flees my lungs. My muscles burn. The stitch in my side overpowers the last of my adrenaline. I crawl up into a tree to hide. This slows my time, but I can't risk him finding me. I ran fast and must have left a trail. Yondin is young, but still a good hunter. He can still find me. Overpower me. Do what he wants with me.

The sun sets and I hold my breath in the growing darkness. Wind from the plains rustles leaves and foliage around me, but over it crackles subtle steps. I grip the rough bark, heart thudding in my ears, as a figure breaks from the foliage as darkness blankets it.

It follows my broken trail, but I can't see who it is. This is only the second day of the hunt. I have so many to go if I want to make it. I breathe in through my nose. Kai and I discussed this. This is the most dangerous timeframe. If I can last until the cove, I'll be fine. My fingers itch to smooth over the seal cloak he left for me. It's more than agreed, but I'm not ungrateful. I bite my cheek, refusing to consider what a good hutmate he'll make someone. But not me. Jokinah.

The figure approaches the base of my hiding tree and disappears back into the bush. I let out a held breath, but my heart stops when another emerges following the first. It's not unheard of for hunters to work together to bring down catches. Sometimes in groups of three or four. They each agree on who they get, but that's sometimes how the fights start too. Still, two is better than one.

I swallow as the second figure follows the trail of the first.

Silence.

I wait and a voice cries out, but not a man's. Sliding down I grip my spear and follow with caution through the foliage. Their trail leads me to the tree line and out onto the flat land of the plains. A hunter kneels over a woman. A catch. I bite my lip.

Nearly full, the moonlight shines down on Yondin as he wraps his hide rope around delicate wrists and ankles. A glint of blonde in the weak light. Jokinah. I run my hands down the smooth sealskin Kaidin gave me. I have to hold up my end of things. I set down my bag of supplies and tighten my white-knuckle grip on the spear. I have one chance to get this right.

Jokinah moans as he rolls her onto her back. Yondin glances over his shoulder, right in my direction, but sees nothing in the shadows I hide in beyond the tree line. He loosens his skins so they sag to his knees. This isn't uncommon either. Many hunters can't wait until their ceremony to take the woman they capture.

But still I wait.

He moans and I slink down the tree line so I can see him. Jokinah's eyes widen, light in the moonlight, as he grips himself above her. Now he pulls on the ties of her split skirt, pushing it away from her hips. Her thighs naked in the moonlight.

I launch myself from the tree line while he tugs on his prick, head thrown back and eyes closed. The butt end of my spear strikes him in the back and he topples over before he can penetrate her. I kick him off balance and he rolls off Jokinah, caught up in his loosened skin wrap. She gasps as I loosen the knot around her wrists.

"Oof—" he knocks me down, tumbling over her.

"Lendhi," he pants, straddling my stomach, pinning my arms with his full weight.

I have trouble breathing beneath him. His hand wraps around my throat, squeezing. He's not trying to kill me, I know this, but he's trying to knock me unconscious.

"Two for one," he smiles down at me. "You're so much trouble but," he leans down, his breath warm on my cheek, whispering into my ear, "You're worth it."

I wrench my shoulders, trying to free myself, turning my face away from his. He licks my cheek.

Jokinah appears behind him, striking the blunt end of a spear against his temple. He slumps forward, his weight pressing me into the earth. I wriggle and she stands behind him, rolling him away. I gasp for air and turn over, coughing. She shakes, holding my spear. I sit up and we both watch as Yondin moans. We tense, but he stays down. She lets out a held breath and offers me her hand. I take it and stumble to my feet, head spinning for a moment. She returns my spear and searches for her own. In silence we put ourselves back together and stand, watching Yondin sleep under the moon. Thank the Seer he breathes.

"So, you decided an honest go at it?" I ask.

She nods.

"Good on you," I turn back to the tree line. She follows me and watches as I retrieve my supplies. She shoulders her own bag, glancing back at Yondin.

"Think he'll be okay?" she asks.

I shrug and push through the foliage into the shadows. She trails me.

"I think so. I'm not worried."

"Are you sure?"

I pause to glare back at her, "I won't tell if you won't. Do you really want to hang around and make sure he wakes up?"

She shakes her head. We continue.

It does worry me. A lot, but I tell myself over and over I'm not the one who did it. I can't condemn myself and my little family in case he's fine and wakes up.

I don't say anything, and neither does she, as we travel through the night. I snap at her about how she walks, leaving a trail, while I tread with care. Without a word she adjusts and we move on. I think nothing of our traveling together. I'll keep her with me in hopes Kaidin finds her. I have to keep up my end of our deal. She can help me stay safe and I can keep her safe for Kai.

At daybreak we take to the trees, fastening ourselves to the branches so we don't fall in our sleep, and rest.

Day Four

We reach the Hollowed Tree at daybreak on the fourth day.

In the thickest part of the forest, where few people ever trek, we're both weary from walking all night and food is getting scarce. I have to share the rations Kai left me with her. I imagine her starving will upset him. It's difficult to gather food effectively and keep up this pace. Now I'm trying to figure out a way to get my cache without rousing suspicion from her. There's no avoiding it I think.

Jokinah follows me in silence. We talk little, but once we find ourselves in the ancient tree's shadow she speaks.

"Here?" she leans on her spear.

The Hollowed Tree stands out from the rest

of the palm forest and bamboo surrounding it. Its large base is the size of a hut. Branches stick out chaotic, every which way from the gnarled trunk. With no leaves, this tree died ages ago. The bark turned black and looms against the rest of the forest greenery. Bush and foliage, and even other trees, give it wide berth. A chill crawls up my spine as I approach the gaping mouth at the base of the tree. It looks like it's screaming.

"First Deer Cave and now here? What is it with you and haunted dwellings?" she doesn't follow me in.

"They're safe," I throw over my shoulder.

"Safe," she stays in place. "From people maybe. Don't anger spirits, Lendhi."

I want to reply with something quick or smart, but I dare not. Air grows cold as I cross the threshold. This place is heavy with the past. All the same, my heart flutters back to life when I find disturbed earth. Signs of Kai. I smile, retrieving a bundle from the pile of dead palm leaves.

We're meant to sleep here, but I step out of the Hollowed Tree, carrying the bundle.

Jokinah cocks her brow, "And what's that?"

I inhale, resisting the urge to dig around in the new bundle.

"I have something to tell you," I grip it and walk past the haunted tree. I want as much space between myself and it as possible. Jokinah trails me. "I have help."

"Help?" her voice is neutral. Nonchalant. Not outraged as I expect.

"It's not against the laws," I offer her silence. That I know of.

I stop and round to face her. She halts and keeps her spear in hand.

"Of course," she says. "We're helping each other, are we not?"

"This help is from a hunter."

Now her blue eyes widen, "What?"

"It's not against the laws," I repeat.

Her gaze wanders to the thicket of the forest, landing on me again.

"It's not. I think. It's just—"

"What?" my heart hammers in my chest. Seer please don't let her turn on me. I really don't want to beat up the mother of Kaidin's future children.

Her lips quirk, "Unheard of."

"Until now."

"Until now," she nods.

I turn back round and we continue on our trek.

"Where are we going?" she asks.

My bones ache. I'm tired. I know she is too.

"We can stop here," I glance up to the thick canopy, trying to gauge a good sleeping tree.

"Yes, but, where are we going? What's our destination?"

"What makes you so sure," I begin climbing a tree as she does. "That we have one?"

"This isn't random wandering. This is a set path. Your friend wouldn't know where to leave your goodies if you didn't have one."

Fair. I blush in my failure at deception, "True. Anaki's Cove."

She disappears into the branches of a tree close to mine.

We don't speak more of it.

Day Five

Rain is an unforgiving tyrant as we traverse the forest. It pours in torrents, forcing us to travel by day, but I wager a hunter can't see any better than we can in this mess. I wrap the sealskin cloak around myself, keeping warm and dry. I imagine Kai walking this same path. Going through this effort.

Jokinah walks beside me and for a moment I'm jealous. What a fine hutmate Kai will make her. He's gone through so much to have her.

"So," I break silence. "What are your plans?"

She startles, walking next to me, and blinks rain drops from her long lashes.

"What? What do you mean?"

I cock my brow, "I mean for the Hunt. What are you wanting to get out of it? I want to be a hunter. Take care of my sister and her runts. What do you want to do if you last the year?"

"Oh," she holds her deerskin cloak over her head. "I don't know if I should say."

"Suit yourself," I push past a thick brush, letting delicate branches slide past me so they don't break. Jokinah trails me in the same fashion. I don't worry about footprints. The rain will wash them away.

"I don't want a hutmate," she pauses. "Well, not…not one that can hunt me."

"What?"

Jokinah swallows, "Never mind."

I feign apathy, mulling over what those words mean as we travel. Silence once again blankets us.

Day Eight

Ocean aroma reaches us before we see the cove. Gulls cry over the waves I know crash against rocks. In the thicket of the forest, sweat rolling down my back, I force myself to slow. We arrive at Anaki's Cove, but we're not safe. We won't be for many days to come.

We stop at the edge of the tree line, staying within its cover, and Jokinah sidles up next to me to peer out from the brush.

A bright high sun shines down over the serene landscape. Sand glistens white beneath aqua green waves crashing into white foam along the smooth shore. Black rock dots the beachline and water sprays over the boulders. Anaki's Cove curves round in a perfect half circle before the beachline disappears round the bend on both sides. My heart stutters in my chest when I spot a lean-to structure half hidden further down the tree line from us. There are stragglers who live on the island who aren't members of the village. I can only hope it's abandoned.

Jokinah's gaze follows mine and spots the lean-to. We both hold our breath. The ocean breeze cools the sweat rolling down my face and neck. My pack is heavy. My feet hurt. I'm so tired and ready to relax, but fear holds me upright. I set down my belongings and garner Jokinah's attention. I motion with my hand for her to stay put as I approach. She nods and sets down her own things, gripping her spear. I take hold of mine and sneak down the tree line towards the lean-to.

I take into account how smooth the sand surrounding it is. No recent activity. The large palm leaves scattered in a careless pile around it might have hidden it well at one time, but wind blew them aside. Getting close, I spot a sealskin pack covered in a light layer of sand. The roof of the lean-to hides the pack from the ocean's side and sand drifted up against the bottom of it.

I break from the brush with my spear in a white knuckle grip and slide down into the lean-to. I shift the palm leaves away and brush the sand off of the cache to open it and peer inside. I crawl out and wave to Jokinah. As I dig through the bag while she approaches, I catch sight of a small patch of light tanned hide inked with writ-speak. I don't speak written very well, but I know the symbols for Kai and return. It's enough.

Kaidin will come back here.

I tuck it out of sight before Jokinah sidles up next to me and sits under the lean-to.

Guilt heats my face while we clear away debris and sand from the shelter. I can't deny how perfect it is we found each other. Kai will see I have her waiting for him. I can return home with pride knowing I held up my end of the bargain, but I'll sacrifice her happiness in exchange.

I frown at the supply cache. She doesn't have nieces and nephews to concern herself with. Jokinah is the eldest daughter of a wealthy family. I don't wish her unhappiness, but I can't risk my sister's runts starving either.

Day Thirty-Five

I keep track of passing days with strikes on a smooth rock I find in one of the streams pouring into the cove.

My finger drags over the marred surface as I count the days since our arrival.

"Twenty-seven," I call out.

Jokinah sits under the shade of the lean-to, hiding from the warm afternoon sun, as she guts a fish to cook over the fire.

We expanded the lean-to for more room, since Kai had only me in mind when he made it, but keep ourselves hidden. We dig a pit down so we don't sit level with the ground and a fire pit in the middle for warmth and cooking. I make a scratch for the day into the rock with a sharpened seal bone knife. In the first week of exploration we found a rotting seal corpse washed ashore and made use of what we could. Carving, I watch Jokinah, a smile playing at my lips as I think of all the hunters who lament over losing her. She is the prize catch this hunt.

In addition to making ourselves more comfortable, we set aside rations to refresh once a week with surplus in case we need to make a quick escape. We decide on a meeting place in case we separate. It's nice to have company, but guilt eats away at any good feelings I harbor about our companionship.

At sunset we sit by the pit of the lean-to, eating next to the dying embers of our cook fire. We try not to have one lit after dark for fear of being spotted.

"I don't want to live like Banki," Jokinah

stops eating and stares at her cooked fish.

I blow on mine, raising my dark gaze to hers.

"I never set out to be a hunter myself," she continues. "But I think that's how I might end up."

"Whatever you want to say, just say it." I bite into my hot meat, sucking air. I swallow, "It's on your mind. I won't tell."

She takes a deep breath, setting down her fish on the palm woven plate.

"I'm in love with Ankhi."

I raise my brows, and thank the Seer my mouth is full. I chew for longer than necessary so I can come up with my reply.

Ankhi lives in Banki's hut, but she doesn't service the hunters like most of the women there. She had a hutmate last Hunt, but he gave her up to get another at this one. You can have more than one hutmate as a hunter, but many hunters can't provide for that many. At the time we assumed, Mirana and I, that she can't have babies. Being given up is the biggest shame a catch can have. Given up to live with Banki.

Now I'm wondering if it's something else that drove Ankhi to live with Banki.

"You want her as your hutmate?" I take another bite.

She nods.

"That's against writ-speak," I say through a mouthful of food as though she doesn't already know.

"She loves me too," Jokinah puts her face in her hands. "I shouldn't have told you."

I sigh and set down my food. Guilt destroys my appetite.

"That's what you meant at the Hollowed Tree," I roll my leftovers up in a palm leaf. "You don't want any of the men."

"Yeah. I don't think I can...do...what I have to. If I'm caught I'll go against everything I feel is me. I want to live with Ankhi. I want to be in her arms at night. Not under some sweaty hunter who only wants to rut and eat."

I can't help but think Kai isn't like that. He wouldn't be. He would be good to her.

Instead, I say, "You love who you love. There's no controlling that."

Her light eyes widen in the growing darkness.

I shrug, "It can't be helped, can it?"

"You won't...turn me in?" she rolls up her fish in palm leaf.

I tuck the sides of the palm leaf inward to keep the fish wrapped as calmly as I can. Does she know?

"What do you mean?"

"Turn me in to the elders...to Perst," she takes my wrapped fish and nudges them together into a basket I wove out of bamboo.

"Oh, no. No, I don't care about any of that."

She quirks a smile and nods.

"I'll tell you something then," my stomach churns with fear and courage. "Kaidin is the hunter helping me."

Her jaw slacks with an intake of breath. I laugh, but it dies quickly.

She swallows, "Kaidin? Really?"

"Yeah. In exchange for his help my sister and I are giving him a set of our fine baskets for a hutmating gift."

"Those baskets are beautiful," she mumbles. "My mother wants some."

"Which is you," I pause. She looks up at me. "Or, it was supposed to be you." I sigh and rub my hands over my face. "But I can't do it to you. Not now."

"Do what?" she places the lid on the bamboo basket.

"I'm supposed to send you his way. I thought if I kept you with me he'll find me and then, you." I raise my hands and shake my head as her muscles tighten. Ready to leap. "No. No. I wasn't going to do anything else. He can get you on his own."

She relaxes, "He's very capable."

"He's coming back. Here. He left writ-speak for me saying so. I don't know when, but I want to be on the lookout. I won't tell him you're here. Not anymore."

She stares down into the dying embers of the fire. The lit coals reflect in her eyes.

"Why? Why work with him?"

"Because Kai isn't like the others. He's kind. A good hunter. He'll make a great provider. He's smart. There's more to him than rutting and eating, as you put it. I think he'll be a good hutmate for you."

Her smile is wry, "Sounds to me you think he'll be a good one for you."

Heat rushes to my cheeks and I frown.

"No."

"No?" she asks.

"He wants you. He said so."

She leans over and takes the hollowed coconut filled with water hanging from the frame of the lean-to and turns it over to douse the embers.

Steam hisses and rises between us.

"You didn't say you don't want him."

"I don't," I lie. "And you know, as well as I, what we want matters little."

The steam thins and her light stare bores into me.

"I do," she says.

I stir the wet embers with a stick, "Think about it though? I'm not asking you to fall in love with him, but Kai is reasonable. If you have to get caught, he's the best you can do. Just think about it."

"All right," she surprises me. "I'll think about it."

I don't know why I'm disappointed.

Day Fifty-Two

As I carve the forty-fourth mark on the counting rock a twig snaps behind me.

I whirl around in time for the butt end of a spear to make contact with my temple. It knocks the breath from me when I fall back into the pit of our lean-to. I gasp, clutching the damp sand as I crawl out. My voice catches in my throat. Hands grab my ankles and bind them in hide rope. Then they yank me back down into the pit, but I reach out towards the sea where I know Jokinah fishes.

And I'm lost to the world of dreams.

When I wake I moan with throbbing pain jittering around my skull.

Tears sting my eyes as I open them. Darkness overhead. Sky beyond the canopy of trees twinkles with the Seer's children. My ancestors. Coated in a layer of sand, I strain my bound wrists behind me. I wriggle my legs to test the strength of knotted rope around my ankles and it has no give. I bite my lip, forcing my heart back down into my chest as I search the darkness.

There's nothing. Only the brush and insects buzzing.

I lay back, my breath short, and close my eyes.

Soft footfalls nearby.

"…got back. I know she's there, but I didn't see her," a masculine, familiar voice says.

I hold my breath, listening for a response.

"She's there. Has to be. They were together."

That's Yondin. Who's he talking to?

"Right, when they beat you up," the other voice chuckles.

I refrain from crying out. Renhin.

"It wasn't a fair fight," Yondin whines. "Anyway, I showed you their trail. I get Jokinah. I want her."

"Then have her. I got what I came for."

The bush next to me rustles and I feel eyes on me as I lay still, trying to feign sleep.

"You need to help me find her," Yondin stands close.

"I don't *need* to do anything," Renhin's baritone cuts through the night as it raises. He must be standing right next to me. "I helped you track them. You can take a little girl by yourself."

"Renhin…"

"Ugh," my captor crouches next to me. His touch through my hair is gentle. "Fine."

I fight the urge to cringe.

"Let me clean her up and we'll go."

"Thanks," Yondin's further away.

"Don't know why you want her anyway," Renhin's skins rustle and I fight to stay still as I imagine the worst happening. Is he unwrapping himself to take me? Should I try to run? Instead, he lays something cool and soothing over my temple. His warm breath blows over my neck as he leans over me.

"What?" Yondin sounds near. "It's Jokinah. Of course I want her."

"She's more likely to rut with your sister than you," Renhin chuckles next to my ear. "And her family aren't good breeding stock."

"And Lendhi's is?"

"Mirana gave Pandin two sons in three years. And," his hand trails down from my head over the curves of my body to my hips. "Look at her. Seer, I can't wait to have her."

His hand squeezes the supple flesh of my hips and thighs as the herbs of the pack seep into my skin. Relief washes over the pounding of my head and I find myself thinking more clearly. I moan and shift.

"And Lendhi's a fighter," Renhin continues running his hands over me. It doesn't seem overtly sexual. More like he's checking for injuries. "She'll defend my children like a cat during a raid."

Yondin chuckles from close by.

"She would."

Renhin lifts the herb pack from my temple and replaces it with another. Another wash of relief.

"I didn't meant to hit her," regret laces his voice. "But she turned. I meant only to knock her off balance."

As I lay pretending to dream I consider my future. Renhin is handsome. A good hunter, but he has cruelty where Kaidin has kindness in his eyes. In fact, I recall Kaidin being at odds with Renhin most of our childhood and even snippets of that rivalry now. Renhin won't help provide for my sister and her runts. He's the worst. He's…I can't quite recall what he is exactly, but he's done many bad things. I'm told. I have to find a way out of this.

"Why don't you have her now?" Yondin asks.

Renhin's hesitation scares my heart into pounding against my temples. I moan and shift again.

"I want to look her in the eyes," he answers, quiet. Almost a whispering caress. "I want to feel her nails on my back. Her cries as I bring her to squeeze in my ear."

"You're waiting until the ceremony? Take her in the mating hut?"

"Perhaps. Perhaps not. It's not any of your business. Maybe instead of focusing on my catch, you should go make yours."

I bite the inside of my cheek, willing this conversation to be over as my thoughts drown out the lull of their voices. I know Renhin wants me. He traveled far and long to find me. There's no doubt. When Mirana's hutmate, Pandin, took her, she hated him. She fought him at first, after their ceremony, and he hit her. Time and again. They lost their first babe in the womb because of it. She caught another child soon after and she changed. She played nice for him. She did as he asked. She complied. Her fear of losing another child and absolute horror when he set his sights on me whipped her into what he wanted. It broke my heart to witness. That's my future with Renhin, I think. I can play it smart from the start or I can fight it and be whipped.

My stomach churns. I want neither.

Tears beyond my control spill from my closed eyes. I want Kaidin. I love Kaidin. I should have told him. I think I've always loved him. I wouldn't mind being a hutmate if it was with someone I love. Now it's too late. He'll have Jokinah. Renhin will have me. And only the men will be happy. As always.

Day Fifty-Three

Renhin's gentle touch puts me to real sleep along with the lull of their idle conversation. It went from talking about my potential as a hutmate to the best way to skin a seal in a hurry.

I wake with the light of day, in the same place on the forest floor, my limbs numb. Moaning, I roll over onto my side and blink up at the brilliant morning sky past the canopy. I hope Jokinah's safe. I hope Kai, at least, finds her if anyone does. My stomach growls and I cough, trying to sit up. When I do my head swims, an herb pack sliding off my temple to land in my lap, and I lay back down. My face twists with a dry sob.

I failed. I failed my sister and her children.

Movement in the brush snaps my attention to rustling foliage. Renhin emerges and Yondin after him, with Jokinah bound and unconscious over his shoulder. Renhin offers me a smile, rising my detest for him, as he crouches close to me. He reaches out and I flinch.

"Shh, shh," he touches the wound on my temple. I can't move away from him and he caresses my cheek. "Easy. I didn't mean to hit you so hard. Don't move unless you have to. Here," he reaches into his pack unslung from his shoulder and pulls out a fresh herb pack. He pours water over it to mix the paste before laying it over my wound. He retrieves the one that slid off and replaces it in his bag.

I bite my lip as the sting from the paste is overtaken by soothing cold.

Renhin smiles and pushes my dark hair from my face. His fingers catch in the tangles and he slips them free.

"We'll get you cleaned up soon," he ties up his pack.

Yondin lays Jokinah with care close to me. Her sleeping form rolls over. He straightens up and glances from me to her and back while Renhin goes to the brush to retrieve a few more weapons and another pack.

"I think I want Lendhi," Yondin grips his spear. "I think you're right about Jokinah."

Renhin keeps his back to Yondin, but he withdraws a dagger from his belt, gripping it with white knuckles.

"No," Renhin says over his shoulder, his voice calm. "We made a deal. Stick to it."

Against the wishes of the Seer I dare hope for a fight. I can use it to get away. I force myself to sit up, head swimming, and meet Yondin's gaze. I knock my knees causing my split skirt to slide and reveal my upper thigh. Mirana uses this often to coddle men out of their extra goods for trade. Yondin doesn't miss it and wipes his mouth with the back of his hand.

"I want Lendhi," he keeps his heated gaze on me like a fool.

Renhin turns, keeping his knife hidden, and drops the packs with his spear. His gaze flickers to me before focusing on Yondin.

"She's mine," Renhin snatches Yondin's attention from me. "I don't want Jokinah. I want Lendhi. You can't have her. You don't have to take Jokinah. I'm sure it would suit her, but you can't have Lendhi."

Their eyes lock. Seeing my chance for escape, I inch backwards before remembering Jokinah, bound and gagged next to me. The two hunters begin circling each other. Yondin withdraws a bone knife from his hip. Renhin's older. More experienced. He fights in many raids to defend our island and attack others. Yondin is strong, young, but lacks the knowledge of a real fight. He's only just old enough to be a hunter in his own right. His hut is still new.

"Back off," Renhin snarls, showing his teeth. "I will kill you for her."

Yondin pauses.

I scooch back and lean against the trunk of a close tree. My stomach churns. I want neither of them to win. Jokinah's chest raises and falls in the dreamland.

"Our mothers are sisters," Yondin says.

"Which is why I haven't killed you yet," Renhin pulls his knife out from behind his back and tosses it with skill, catching it by the handle. "And that's why I helped you get Jokinah."

Yondin bows his head, casting his eyes downward.

"You're right. Sorry."

Yondin turns and glances at me before bending down, knife in his grip. He spins to throw it at Renhin, but my captor's quick, his knife disappearing into Yondin's ribs. Yondin cries out and drops his knife, not having a chance to throw it, falling to his knees, blood spilling over the forest floor. Moss and dead leaves soak it up.

I cry out and kick my feet to scoot away.

Renhin stands over Yondin's moaning form. It isn't a fatal wound, but painful. Renhin adjusts his grip on the knife and crouches next to Yondin.

"Don't," tears spill down my cheeks. "Leave him be."

"If I wanted him dead, he would be," Renhin looks down at me with blood covered hands. "You plead for him?"

"He's so young," I say. Yondin curls up, pressing his hand against the wound. "Stupid."

Renhin smiles and wipes the blade of his bone knife on Yondin's hide wrap. He stands and approaches me.

"He would have taken you weeks ago. Not shown you the same mercy. He wouldn't treat you well."

"How," I lick my lips and his eyes drop down to my naked thigh. I shift my legs, curling them inward, "Are you any different?"

To my surprise, he frowns and sighs. Shakes his head.

"How is your head?" he crouches close to me. I pull away from his touch and he places his hand on the back of my neck, forcing me to still. "You seem better."

I can't stand his intense blue gaze and choose to watch Yondin's writhing form. He breathes, but blood seeps out.

"I'm fine," I swallow.

"Good," Renhin reaches out for me and in one fluid motion has me over his shoulder. He stands and I wriggle in his grasp. He rests his hand on my ass to hold me in place while grabbing his things with the other. He leaves Yondin's packs behind with their owner.

"We can't leave them like this," I cry as he turns from the clearing and presses into the brush.

"Of course we can," he carries me. "He'll recover soon."

"Jokinah!" I pull against my restraints. Please Seer, let her hear me. "Jokinah!"

Renhin chuckles, vibrating against my stomach over his shoulder.

"I'm not going to take her so she can give you pleasure while I'm away."

I want to call him a fool. She doesn't care for me as she does Ankhi, but I know better. I know that if I'm smart, and I am, I'll never call Renhin a fool again.

Day Fifty-Six

It's hard to keep count of time as the sun flies over us, but we reach the plains and Renhin sets me down. He pants and a sheen of sweat layers his bare torso. I lay back in the grass and watch the sky purple with sunset.

He unties the rope at my ankles and kneels behind me to loosen the rope binding my wrists.

I rub my wrists and ankles, my limbs numb, before jumping to my feet. I turn to run, but stumble and fall into the grass. He laughs.

"Lendhi," he retrieves salted fish from his pack and offers it to me.

I'm starving, so I take it, eating.

"If you're good for me, I'll be good for you."

Nodding I focus on the fish. It's a fair trade hunters make with their catches. Not that many of them abide by it, but I can't expect less.

"If you're not," he continues. "I'll punish you." His frightening words lack conviction.

I glance up to his cold gaze.

"I'll never get rid of you. I'll not cast you to Banki's hut. Nor will I kill you, but I will punish you."

I swallow.

"I'll let you give your sister a basket of food a week."

My mouth slacks. He reaches up and tucks his finger under my chin to shut it gently.

It's not enough, but it's a start. Perhaps if I do his bidding I can provide for my family after all. My heart sinks. I feel like I'm betraying Kai by considering this, but why?

"You'll not get such a kind offer from anyone else," he says.

Kai will offer it, if he has any interest in me, which he doesn't. Renhin's right. I hate it, but I'm not his until we cross the threshold of the village. Whether he lays with me or not. The ceremony has to be done before I'm officially his hutmate.

"All right," I force myself to say. "I'll think about it."

He smiles.

I smile back and ignore burning in the back of my throat as I eat fish.

Day Fifty-Nine

While we walk through the forest Renhin doesn't bother tying me up. He's confident he can catch me again. He's in no rush to return either and we take an indirect path towards the village. He ties me up when he hunts for food, always hidden and within earshot. He doesn't want another hunter to find me. I don't either, so I stay still and quiet.

He returns soon with an entire deer. He has skill. I can't deny it. He's handsome too. I can't deny that either. When I begin to feel warmth towards him his cold blue gaze drowns it.

In the evening he unties me again and starts a fire. It burns high and bright in a clearing between the trees and brush. I relish the warmth of the flames. With Renhin I don't have to worry about hunters coming for me. There's no one to hide from.

My captor watches me past the flames, eating. I keep to myself and do the same, weighing my options. He offers to help my sister, though not enough, but he offered without prompting. Which is promising. I remain grateful, and surprised, he hasn't rutted me yet. I know it's a matter of time though. Even if he takes me by force, I'm not his until after the ceremony. Most hunters don't want a catch who's spoiled, but I can't become a hunter myself either if he takes me and doesn't claim me as a hutmate.

I frown. What a stupid word. Spoiled. I'm not a fish or water well gone bad. I can't be spoiled.

I can run or let him have me, then run. If I let him have me no one else will want me, but I'll go back to the same existence I share with Mirana in our dilapidated hut. Which, was it really so bad? It is if we end up in Banki's hut. Ankhi might get away without servicing hunters, it's doubtful Mirana and I can. My nephews will come of age, but that's many spins around the sun away. And if I let Renhin rut me, a baby can catch. I'd rather be under his watchful eye, my belly full, with child than alone and free with it. After seeing what Mirana went through with her babies, the thought of doing it in that old hut and starving is enough to anchor me to Renhin.

His eyes follow my every movement as I eat.

"Do you know what the squeeze is?" he sets down his meat to let it cool.

I startle, holding a hot piece of juicy meat up to my mouth, but lower it. Blood rushes to my cheeks. His intense gaze is hard to look into, and so I watch the dancing flames of the fire.

"Yes," I whisper.

He nods, picking up his food, "I'm going to make you do it." He takes a bite.

I gasp, my heart thudding in my chest.

The squeeze is when a man can bring a woman to great pleasure. My sister, and others who live with Banki, say it's wise to fake one for a man. Most hunters don't notice, and most who notice don't care. I have a feeling Renhin will care. Mirana faked many squeezes for Pandin, to keep him happy. To make him believe he rutted well. Women who live with Banki are always happy to go into detail about it. I know very well what it is.

I curl my legs to tuck under myself and set down the meat. Steam rises off of it. Renhin smiles past the flames, making my stomach churn. What a declaration!

My feet itch to run. I don't understand his focus on me, or his patience. I've known Renhin most of my life and by known I mean known of him. My interactions with him are rare and infrequent. I didn't realize he knew I existed, much less picked me out for his hutmate. This is the most I've spoken with him and now it's about him making me squeeze.

I cover my hot cheeks.

What's worse is…I'm not repulsed by the idea. I flicker my gaze up to meet his. I entertain coupling with him for the first time. Letting the imagery fill my mind. How his large hands might feel…I haven't given up, but I must consider all options for the future.

"A blush for me?" his eyes drop to my heaving chest for the first time. Cold in his eyes dissipates into warmth. No, not warmth, but blazing heat.

I hug myself and frown. My brows furrow at his correct assumption.

"So pure," he mutters, stoking the fire with a stick. Almost to himself. "Unlike the women of that house you grew up in."

My silence encourages him.

"That's good. Not that it'll change my mind if you aren't."

I rub my thighs together and keep my arms wrapped around my middle. I don't like how he makes me feel. I don't want to feel like this. Not with him, of all people.

"Why me?" I dare to look him in the eye. "Why am I the one?"

Renhin drops his gaze to the fire, "Wouldn't you like to know?"

As time drags by, he says no more.

I'm positive he sleeps.

Crickets chirp in nearby brush. We're close to the tree line and this is my best chance. He's gotten comfortable, and while I'm still bound, I managed to flex out my wrists enough when he tied me earlier tonight. Behind my back I push and pull and yank until one of my hands slips free with discomfort. I wince, flexing my fingers in front of me. Renhin sleeps with his back to me. Probably because he doesn't see me as a threat, and he's right. He's a light sleeper. I have to be careful.

I watch his even breath; his lungs expand and constrict in sleep. Or what I hope is sleep. I allow myself a moment to stare at his muscular back openly. His offer appeals to me. Especially when I think of the other hunters who might have an interest in me. Renhin isn't the worst option. If Pandin was alive he would have been one. I cringe. My poor sister.

I have to try. As tempting as Renhin's offer is, it's not as good as my freedom. Being a hunter myself. Or, in the very back of my mind repressed by jealousy, being Kai's hutmate.

My eyes never leave his sleeping form as I free myself. I loosen the binding around my ankles, his knots are hard to untie, and unweave the hide rope. Embers of the dead fire crackle and residual heat rises in waves between us. Searching for anything I can use in the bush, I find nothing within arm's reach and I don't dare get closer to him. I rub feeling back into my legs before jumping to my feet. A cool breeze blows loose strands from my braid, tickling my face. I hold my breath, watching him. I take my first step back onto the grass. The soft ground assists in keeping me quiet as I back away, facing him, up to the foliage of the tree line.

He bolts upright, searching, his eyes snapping to me in an instant before I turn and disappear into the brush. I have no destination, or even direction, in mind as my legs pump, my feet pounding into the soft carpeting of moss and dead leaves beneath the canopy. Moonlight doesn't filter through the thick canopy as I run and darkness forces me to slow down and reach out, hoping to find any low hanging branches with my palms instead of my face.

"Lendhi!" he's too close behind me.

Panic surges me forward, reckless, into the dark foliage. My foot catches on a root and I stumble before tumbling head over heels, landing face first. The carpet of the forest floor helps to break my fall, but I cry out in frustration.

Renhin stands over me in an instant.

I gasp and crawl forward, away from him, and he grabs my ankle to drag me backwards. His strength is terrifying and alluring.

"I won't lie," he flips me over onto my back, sitting on my stomach to pin me. The bastard isn't even panting. "I would have been disappointed in you if you didn't try."

Gritting my teeth and gasping for air, I fist my hands and try to hit him. He snatches my wrists and holds them, but still I struggle, wriggling my legs and yanking to fight his grip. He grips my wrists in his large hand and slides down from my waist to sit over my hips. The intimate placement stills me and I swallow, blood rushing to my cheeks.

He leans over, pinning my wrists above my head on the ground. His lips press against mine. The kiss starts slow and lazy. Cold before fire ignites in him and his mouth consumes mine, finding my lips pliant to his force. His tongue sweeps into my mouth, stealing my breath.

I hate how it makes me feel. How his touch spurs my body to want him. Desperately. How can my mind and body war so? How can they be so out of tune? But I react to him, whether I like it or not. I can't hold back as my lips move against his. I whimper as he settles his weight over me, his hand travels down, releasing my wrists, to the curve of my hip. I claw my fingers into the mixture of upturned sand and leaves above my shoulders. He rolls onto his side, and I can escape if I jump, but I don't move.

Instead I tremble and lay still as his warm hand slides down under the waist of my skirt. He studies my face and I bite my lip, gasping, while his fingers brush against the heat between my legs.

With a heated stare he leans in, pressing his lips to my neck. The warmth of his body contrasts the cool night air as his thumb finds my swollen nub and rubs it. My face twists in blissful agony as fire ignites in my gut. Oh Seer, I want him.

"After our ceremony," his husky voice murmurs against my skin. "I'm going to fuck you everyday for the rest of our lives."

I shake my head and arch my back as his finger dips into my eager body. Too quickly it grows slick.

"No," I manage between moaning and crying out. "No."

He chuckles, "No?"

I yelp as he curls his finger, brushing against something inside me to make my legs tremble. My muscles tighten around his touch as my body grows taught. I can't breathe. I can't think. Only his lips and hands consume me. I want him all over me. In me. A rush of electricity floods my senses and I contract in unspeakable, brief, maddening pleasure. I cry out, arching my back.

As I relax against the forest floor he pulls his wet fingers from between my legs, smearing evidence of my squeeze over the hot skin of my stomach. His eyes never leave mine as he licks and sucks his fingers. I shudder.

"That, was a squeeze," he whispers. "Perhaps next time I can use my tongue." He plants his mouth on my neck and kisses down my collar bone.

"What?" I sit up on my elbows. He comes up with me, pressing me back down to the earth.

He rolls over, his body warm over mine, heavy.

"Shhh," he lays his head on my chest. It raises and falls with my slowing breath.

I blink, my lids heavy. Sudden exhaustion weighs down my body. Cradling his head, I fall asleep on the forest floor.

Day Sixty

I dream of Kaidin kissing me. Pressing me against the trunk of a tree by the stream near our village.

His large callused hands are warm as they remove my deer hide skirt and top. His lips kiss down from my neck to my breasts. Down past my waist.

I wake.

I curl up, alone, with a soft sealskin cloak draped over me. In the night Renhin must have carried me back to our campsite. A new fire burns low. The aroma of cooking makes my stomach grumble. Renhin is out of sight when I sit up to study my surroundings. We're still close to the tree line. The sun shines high in the sky. I overslept. Rubbing my eyes I pull the cloak away and fold it next to me. Movement in the brush and I snap my gaze to find Renhin emerge with a skin sack weighed down with contents.

Seer, he is handsome though. If nothing else.

Especially when he smiles at me like that.

I fight a grin trying to curl my lips as memories of last night stir the heat between my legs. Renhin's promises quicken my heart. A basket a week for my sister. I think I can talk him up to more than that, but I have to play this game carefully. Isn't that what this is about? I'm in the Hunt. There's nothing to be done about it. If I can't become a hunter in my own right, perhaps Renhin is my best chance for a happy life. He's on par with Kai for hunting and ability to provide. Not only for myself, but Mirana and her runts. Otherwise she'll be helpless until her own sons come of age. Assuming they don't die of starvation before then. Or in a raid. Or they go back to live with Banki. Once a woman goes to Banki, the village elders can take her children away.

Renhin sits next to me, instead of across the fire as usual, and opens the sack. He withdraws bright juicy fruit Mirana and I can never afford in the trading market. It grows in the wild, but by the village it's cultivated by wealthy families, like Jokinah's. With his bone knife, Renhin peels away the bright yellow skin with a tint of orange and slices it into several pieces. Juice runs down his hands and forearms. Keeping eye contact with me, he licks the juice from his fingertips to elbow.

Heat rushes to my cheeks as he holds out a slice of fruit.

My mouth waters and I swallow with sudden onset salivation. I don't understand his seduction. He can just, take me. Like all the others. Why doesn't he? I hesitate, reaching out to take the fruit. It's cool and moist, juice dribbling down my hand as I bite into it. I close my eyes. I've not had it before. Juicy and sweet, tangy with a twinge of sour aftertaste.

"Seer," I whisper.

Renhin smiles.

"Sometimes I forget how poorly you live," he carves up the fruit, offering me every other piece as he eats with me.

We finish it in silence.

It is easy for others to forget my hardships. It's easy for me to forget the hardships of others. I focus on the fruit and make a face when the sour hits. Renhin laughs and offers me the last piece. A small smile crawls over my lips. I can't help it. I've never seen him laugh. Not really. Before now, I never saw him smile. Not sincerely. I never thought of Renhin as a person. Or think of any hunters as people. Except for Kai.

We share the meat he cooks over the fire. A quiet, nice meal. As I watch him work I notice his hands. They move slow and deliberate. Dexterous. Blush creeps over my face as I think of how dexterous they were last night. I'm equal parts dreading and anxious for another night like it. I want more, but I keep thinking I should try harder to escape. Like I need to hold out. My plans crumble with each simple gesture of his kindness. With each gentle touch or care taken towards me, my resolve dissipates.

Any memory of his cold eyes as he stabbed Yondin fades with my suspicions of him.

Day Sixty-Two

We're close to the village.

We stay at our campsite for a couple of days. Renhin takes his time. We sit and eat. He hunts. I help prepare food and process hides and bones for later use. He doesn't touch me intimately again and I don't dare ask no matter how desperately I need it. That was a trial, I think. For the real thing. Like this is. This is how we will be when we return to the village. I'm happy with this, but confused. This is nothing like I thought he would be. Especially given our rare encounters before now. Did he talk to Kaidin? Maybe my friend threatened him into being nice. I smile to myself while carving up a wild chicken next to the fire, thinking of how that scenario might play out. Kaidin would do that. I think.

"What are you thinking about?" Renhin watches me work while he relaxes, leaning back on his hands.

Heat rises to my cheeks, "Something funny my nephew did."

He continues to watch me work. Maybe we're both on trial. He said he'll never get rid of me. Maybe he sees me as more than a possession. He takes mating seriously. He wants to make sure I can be a good hutmate too. Then again, nothing stops him from taking many. I hate that I don't understand him.

"You really love them, don't you?" he shifts, leaning forward.

"I do," I carve out the leg and set it on the cook spit, keeping my gaze down on the meat. "I will do anything for them." Including mate with him.

"Lendhi," he tucks his finger under my chin, forcing me to look up into his blue eyes. "I'll tell you what I expect from you. And then you can say what you expect from me. How does that sound?"

I bite my lip, "That sounds good, but why?"

"Why what?" he cocks his brow.

"Why do you care?"

His smile isn't smug, or amused, or a smirk, like I expect. Instead it's wary. Almost pitying.

"I can't tell you all my secrets, but would you rather I didn't care?"

"No," I shake my head. "No, that's not what I mean. I appreciate it."

"I would be suspicious too," he drops his hand. "But I can't divulge everything. What I can tell you is I expect a partner. Not a slave. I want children. I want to embrace you in the night without worry of getting you pregnant or disease."

Heat flushes down my neck and chest. He's thinking of the women who live with Banki. The same kind of women who raised me. The same women who will disappear with a man behind the bush and return with dinner. Renhin enjoyed their company at one time. I'm sure Kai has too. They all have.

He continues, "You can skin and cook. Sell at market. Sew. Even make decent weapons. And, you come from a fertile line. You have no brothers now, but we all know why. I think you'll give me the sons I need. You'll help me build up to become what I'm destined to be. Together. You're my best choice."

It's fair. I can't ask for better, if I have no alternative.

"What do you wish to become?" I ask.

"Chief," he flips over the leg cooking on the spit, shaking his hand from the heat.

My brows shoot up. A very ambitious goal. We haven't had a chief, true tribal leader, in two generations. The line of leaders died out and our elders at the time, with the Perst, couldn't come to a decision about a successor. Now they, the elders and Perst, make all decisions. Including who becomes the next chief. No one proves worthy. The elders and Perst aren't keen on losing their own grasp on power either.

Weight presses down from the blue sky. My stomach churns. He asks no small thing. As a regular hutmate I'll struggle. Birthing is hard. I helped Mirana with all three of her children. Another reason I want to avoid being a hutmate. I want children, but it's frightening.

"And if I refuse?" I ask.

Renhin considers me. His silence draws out.

"You'll best suit my purpose. I will take you anyway, but that's really not how I want it."

I nod. Even if I escape he'll hunt me. He's driven. I have to last the year, and we're not a third of the way through it. He caught me easily. I shouldn't give up, but I don't know how long I can last with him following me. Pursuing. I can't ever stop. He's already proven he'll go to the other end of the island for me. Anaki's Cove was my best chance.

"Why would you refuse?" he asks.

I shrug and carve the breast from the chicken, laying it on the spit. Fat sizzles on hot coals beneath it.

"Fear," I whisper.

"Of what? Me?" he inches closer, staying my hand.

"I'm afraid of many things," I glance at him,

65

resting my hands on the raw meat in my lap. "I'm afraid for my sister. Her children. Your high expectations. What happens when I don't meet them?"

"You already do," his fingers rest over the back of my hand. "I'm not keeping you out here just for your ease of comfort. It's also for mine."

I bite my lip, "There's no guarantee I can give you sons."

He shrugs, "Once I am chief I can take any hutmate. Anytime. If we have no children by the next Hunt, I can try with someone else. But we have chemistry. I can bring you to pleasure and I don't doubt," he leans in close, his lips against my ear sending chills down my spine. "You can bring it to me."

"But," I keep my composure. Barely. "It's difficult to become chief without a son."

He pushes a loose strand of my dark hair behind my ear.

"True, but that's a gamble with any woman. Not just you. I think the odds are in our favor."

Because of my sister and the runts I love like my own. Even my parents had five children in a short of amount of time. Before…

Renhin's blue eyes dance to the tree line before refocusing on me.

My heart thuds in my chest, "What is it?"

"Someone watches us," he speaks soft. "Another hunter."

This close to the village it doesn't surprise me.

I swallow and carve at the remains of chicken, seeking out plump flesh and placing it on the spit. Taking the bone knife, I turn the pieces on it over.

Renhin's bone knife. I know for a fact he is the reason this mystery hunter doesn't approach.

"I'm considering your offer," tears well in my eyes. "But this is what I expect from you. I want more than a basket a week for my sister. I want her and the children to be cared for. Never hungry. Never cold."

He takes a deep breath, his eyes snapping to the tree line. He tenses up, relaxes, and tenses again. His hand wraps around the body of his spear lying next to him. He's ready. For whatever it is he waits for.

"I want to amass wealth," he keeps his focus on the tree line. "Which will prove difficult if we provide for another family."

I frown and his gaze flickers to me. I don't expect my unhappiness to affect his decision, but to my surprise he says, "I'll reconsider it when things get going. Your sister is not without her uses."

He watches the tree line, missing my slack jaw.

I recover, "Do you plan to take her as a second hutmate? Is that possible?"

He chuckles and shakes his head.

"I don't plan to ever take a second hutmate, though it's possible for a hunter to take your sister if he wants her. Her hutmate died. She wasn't cast out. And if it's absolutely necessary for me to take a second hutmate, it won't be her. That's not right."

My brows raise and burning meat grabs my attention. I use the bone knife to stab into a succulent piece of meat and lift it off the spit onto a large waiting palm leaf. I groan as I examine the charred chicken and cut the ruined pieces away. Renhin reaches down to snatch a piping hot piece from my hands, popping it into his mouth. He sucks in air through his teeth, but his eyes remain on the tree line.

"However," he swallows and drinks from the water skin. "It will look good on me, in the eyes of the elders and especially the Perst, to take in your sister and her runts. Wouldn't it?"

I shrug, "I don't know the standards set for chieftain."

"Kindness can be overlooked, but weakness isn't. How much kindness can I show without seeming weak?" He rubs his jaw, his eyes darting between the tree line and the plains around us. My gaze trails down his neck to his muscular chest and abs. He didn't reapply the black paint hunters wear over their torso and arms after it faded. He stays bare, and it must mean something. About this discussion. Perhaps he talks to me as an equal? I'm too imaginative for my own good sometimes. Perhaps he's just too lazy to put it on.

Taking a deep breath, I check the rest of the cooking meat and pull it off the spit. I set to work on cleaning the bones of chicken so they can be used for decoration and weapon pieces.

He continues stealing pieces of hot meat from the leaf while I let it cool and work.

"Will it make you happy?" his blue gaze glances at me from the tree line.

"Yes," my heart skips a beat. "Very happy."

He nods. The meat cools and I eat.

Morning passes in silence as we finish our

meal. Renhin asks me to help him pack up the camp and I do, with a thundering heart. We didn't move for days and I wonder if the mystery hunter in the tree line is responsible. Renhin leads me into the thicket of the jungle, to my surprise, and stops at the stream I know leads a winding path down by the village. Here it is wider and more like a river, flowing quick. I drop to my knees on the soft grassy bank to splash water on my face. Sunlight shines down on the carpet of greenery from the gap in the canopy.

Renhin, who carries everything at his insistence, sets down the packs on the soft grass and looks up to the blue sky with fluffy white clouds. He sits and draws up his knees, resting his elbows on them.

"Maybe we should bathe," he ticks his head towards the running water.

I pause washing my face and arms. Water droplets fall from my lashes as I dare to glance at him over my shoulder. His cool gaze steadies and the side of his mouth curls upward. He cocks his brow.

"Look away," I clear my throat. Swallowing. A bath does sound amazing.

"So you can run while I'm not looking?" he shakes his head. "No. Soon I'll see you anyway. Why not now?"

Heat rises to flush my cheeks and chest. I can't speak. He's not wrong. He stands up, grabbing his spear, and approaches the spring to crouch next to me.

"All right," he strokes my cheek. "I'll do it first." He sets down the spear and stands. I kneel next to him, watching as he loosens the deerskin wrap around his waist. It drops to his ankles.

My eyes dart to the water and I don't think it's possible for my face to redden more. I catch a glimpse of it. It. I force myself to take a deep breath, expanding my lungs. My hands shake as I plunge them into the cool water. The stream bubbles up around my fingers. In my peripheral he steps into the water and begins to bathe himself. I dare to look up, catching his heated blue eyes, watching my every move like a hunter. The hunter he is.

I can't bring myself to look down past his waist.

He crouches next to me. I bite my lip and look away. He tucks his finger under my chin to face him. He leans in, closing his eyes, and his lips press to mine. I hate how much I love them. Warm. Soft. He pulls me against his hard chest and I ball my hands into loose fists and close my eyes. The warmth of his skin contrasts the cool water. I snake my arms around his neck and lean into our kiss. His tongue sweeps into my mouth as his arms crush me against him. Crawling into his lap, my legs circle his waist. He hardens against me. I gasp a little moan as he grinds our hips together.

He pauses, our lips ghosting against each other, sharing our breath, "I won't force you."

I open my eyes to his intense gaze and furl my fingers into his thick blonde hair. Is this it? The moment I think of many times on my own. Alone at night. In my cold bed. Knowing others in the village enjoy what I can only imagine, but dreading it. Wondering if I will be stuck like Mirana. This doesn't feel stuck. This feels good. Right.

I tremble, "I don't know."

He runs his hand along my jaw and smiles,

leaning in and kissing me before he pulls away.

"We'll wait until you do."

It disappoints me he doesn't push further, but I don't show it. Instead, I reach for the ties of my top and stand to slip it off. Then the tie of my split skirt. It pools at my feet and I cover myself with my hands. Trying to hide what he stares at. I allow myself to look down at him. My hands slide to my flat stomach. His blue gaze sweeps over my form and glazes. He's ready for me. He wants me. I want him.

I kneel by the water and he crawls over me, between my legs, pressing me down onto my back. Our kissing turns feverish. Delirious pleasure overwhelms logic and I find myself widening my thighs to cradle him against me. He takes my breath away when he grinds his hips against mine, pressing the girth of his erection against me.

"I want to wait for the ceremony," he murmurs as his mouth travels down my jaw to my neck and collar bone. I claw into his hair as his lips latch over my risen nipple.

"Seer," I squeeze him between my thighs. I forget all my dreams of the future with his fiery lips and touch. He sucks my sensitive skin, sending shockwaves of pleasure down my nerves and between my legs. Hunger consumes me.

His large hands knead the supple flesh of my breasts and hips. He might stop if I ask him to, but I don't. I don't want him to stop.

A dull ache before sweeping pain as he enters me. I clutch his wide shoulders and arch my back, closing my eyes and crying out. I can't get enough air. This is what I want, but my stomach coils as pain penetrates me deeper with him. He moans, his lips against my neck, as he snaps in to the hilt. He trembles, holding himself above me. He stills and allows me time to recover from discomfort. It eases. His steamy breath coats my jaw and he slides his lips up to mine.

"You feel so good," he murmurs against my mouth and jaw.

Pain decreases as we lay, attached, as close as two people can be, in the quiet of the clearing, by the gentle whisper of the stream. Birds chirp in the canopy above, oblivious to this life changing moment. I suck in deep breaths as his hand slides between our bodies to rub my engorged nub. I bite my lip and he begins to move his hips in shallow rhythm. Friction builds between us. Pleasure overpowers the residual aching. He grunts and fists my hair, pulling my head back to shower my neck and breasts with kisses.

His speed increases until the bliss of friction cast by our naked bodies overwhelms me. My face scrunches as I struggle for breath. A loud whining moan erupts from my lips as my muscles contract around his girth. Renhin's teeth nip the skin of my neck and he grunts, snapping himself against me as he warms my insides.

He holds his weight off me, panting, and licking the sensitive skin of my neck where he bit me. I close my eyes, enjoying the warmth. The satisfaction. He softens in me, but doesn't move. Instead, his mouth finds mine and fondness surpasses my surprise. Only for a moment do I wonder what this might have been like with Kaidin. But it flees and Renhin's warmth and attention snap me back to reality.

"Now," he kisses me again. "You're mine."

Insisting, Renhin washes me in the stream. I blush as he strokes and caresses my tender body and sore muscles. I wince as little as possible, but he frowns.

"I'm sorry Lendhi," he kisses my bent knee, sitting in front of me, still naked himself, between my legs. "I planned that differently."

I bite the inside of my bottom lip and shrug.

"It wasn't bad," I say as he stands. I study him openly. He's unashamed of his nudity and really, why should he be? He's handsome.

"It could have been better," he steps onto the soft grass of the embankment. "I could have prepared you better."

"I squeezed," I suck in my breath as I close my thighs. I wait in the bubbling water for my sore muscles to adjust.

He grins lopsided, "You did, but it will be better next time."

Next time. My stomach lurches with anticipation. There will be a next time. And I can't wait.

"You've," I swallow, keeping my eyes down on the water. "Planned this for a while?"

Renhin dresses and begins to set up camp, laying down soft sealskin blankets and prepping an area for a fire.

"Yes."

I nod, "For how long?"

He pauses in thought, "At least four years, but it may be more than that. Four at least."

Four years ago I was sixteen. Mirana was pregnant with her third child, the first having not made it to maturation, and I lived under Pandin's scrutiny and leering gaze. Back then I imagined being free of him. Had I known someone like Renhin waited for, no, planned to take me, I might have run to him. At the time I imagined running away with Kaidin even though we weren't friends anymore. My heart anchors into my stomach as I think of Kaidin. He won't want me now. No chance. No hope. But, he never did, did he? I slide my gaze over to Renhin, who watches me as he piles twigs and wood with fodder.

I didn't like Renhin, but now I do. He isn't Kaidin, but he's enough. I cringe at the thought of settling. I betrayed Kaidin, and my sister and her children, and myself. And yet, I don't really feel that way. It's almost as though I feel obligated to feel that way. I resisted having a hutmate for so long. A future with Renhin, if he truly is like this, and stays like this, will be amazing. I never thought to be happy with someone like Renhin. In the weeks before the Hunt he hinted to wanting me, but I turned away with disgust. He has a reputation. He visited Banki's hut often. The women of the hut never complained of him, though. They never said anything. Good or bad. He's an aggressive warrior during raids. During defenses. He seems cold and distant. He seems so many things I don't see now. Now I see a capable provider. A handsome warrior who will defend me. In place of condescendence I see quiet thoughtfulness. Potential. Perhaps he went through the same process with me. Maybe he watched me. Took the time to see the real me and decided I won't be a bad choice. I don't have the best reputation around the village either. I know people think I'm rough. Too strong willed. Not a pliable hutmate. Four years is a long time for Renhin to think about this. My opinion of him changed in merely days. Weeks? I'm losing track of time.

"Was there someone?" he startles me from my thoughts. "A hunter you wanted to catch you? I know you were training to be your own, but I often wonder."

"Yes," I swallow the lump in my throat.

"Not me," he strikes two pieces of flint together. It isn't a question.

"No, not you."

He nods, his mouth set in a line. Not a scowl, but not a smile. I think he already knows that. He prepared for the answer I gave him.

"You know it's me or no one now, right?" he pauses, keeping his eyes on a wisp of smoke smoldering among the twigs. "They won't want you now."

"I know," I chafe my arms and hug myself, standing by the cool water. I reach down and slide my clothes back on.

The sun disappears below the canopy and we're cast in the shadows of late afternoon.

"I do," he stands and closes the distance between us. "I want you. Whether or not I was the first to take it. I want you."

The warmth of his body shields me from the cool touch of shadows. With the sun gone, darkness dips the temperature around us. He brushes his hand over my cheek.

"Len," he tries an endearing form of my name. "We can make each other happy."

Tears well my eyes. It's too late. To change anything. Kaidin didn't want me to begin with. Now he won't give me a second thought. A second glance.

I launch myself into Renhin's embrace and he squeezes me, resting his chin on the crown of my head. His large hands smooth down my back and shoulders. I don't know why I'm crying against his chest. I don't know why I find him comforting.

But I know why I say, "You're right. I will be your hutmate."

The next time comes in the middle of the night. I wake from slumber, nestling under a sealskin blanket across the dying embers of the fire from Renhin. His breath is even, moving up and down, but the moment I sit up and crawl close to him, it stops. He holds it, listening for what disturbs the air. He sits up. Heat from beneath his blanket escapes and warms me.

"Len?" his voice is rough from sleep.

I slide beneath the blanket beside him. Without prodding he wraps his arms around me and our lips meet. I want more of him. And I get it. I slide my hand down past the waist of his wrap and find him already half ready for me. I bite my bottom lip and he cocks his brow. Our skins move aside and we join, again. I'm so ready for him. Slick and hot. He's right. I can concentrate more on the pleasant feeling than the dull ache accompanying it. He's gentle. Slow. Doing everything I need. He reads my body like writ-speak. Renhin pushes my top up over my breasts and lavishes them with his mouth and tongue. I pull him to me. Hoping he'll devour me with his desire. A burst of happiness flutters my heart as his hips snap to mine again and again. I can have this anytime I want now. For the rest of my life.

We writhe and I squeeze twice for him before he stills inside me. Our shared breath steams the air around us. I fall asleep before we detach.

Day Sixty-Three

I wake from a distant dream of a crying baby. The sun is high over the canopy and our fire burns low with a fresh slab of meat cooking over it. It sizzles as fat drips down onto the flame. Renhin sits close, flipping over the meat. He smiles when I stretch and sit up to rub my lower back.

He leans in and kisses my cheek as I pull my top and skirt back into place.

I blush and rub sleep from my eyes. My hand rests over my abdomen as the dream resurfaces. I had many children, but they were Kai's. Not Renhin's. I frown. That isn't what I want anymore. What a stupid dream. Renhin's blue gaze drops to my hand a moment and his brows raise.

"I dreamt I was pregnant," I drop my hand into my lap.

"Perhaps you are," he laughs as color drains

from my face. "It'll be all right."

This is part of what he wants me for, but I can't help thinking of my sister's struggles through carrying her runts. The one she lost. Her heartache. She hated Pandin, but loves her children. I will be lucky not to hate my hutmate. I may love him in time. But her birthing… My stomach lurches. It seems impossible for something so big to pass through me.

"Len," Renhin grabs my attention. "It'll be all right. I won't let anything bad happen to you."

Nodding, I force a smile. He brushes my cheek. He becomes more familiar with my name, touching me casually, and I'm more comfortable around him. It feels like we've been together a while. Will he really only take me? I remember his parents. Renhin's family is well known in the village, and one of the reasons is because his father took only one hutmate. It's rare for wealthy families to have one hutmate. His father never even visits Banki's hut. One of the few. Will Renhin be the same? I can't be surprised or insulted if he isn't, but now a flight of sparrows flitter in my stomach. Maybe he will be. For the long haul. For forever.

I hope years from now Kaidin will be a distant thought. A fleeting memory of childhood fantasy. I focus on the tangible man before me. The one who wants me. Is willing to fight for me. I allow myself a brief fantasy of Kaidin and Renhin fighting over me. I laugh to myself and shrug away Renhin's quirked brow and half smile.

"Now what?" he asks.

"Can I call you Ren?" I turn to kiss the palm of his hand against my cheek.

He laughs and catches himself, "Of course

you can."

"Len and Ren," I mull it over. "Almost…" I don't dare say this out loud.

But he does, "Meant to be?"

Day Sixty-Five

Apprehension weighs me down as we walk. The village is in sight, sunset casting golden hues from between the trees and brush to wash the huts and walls in its glow.

I slow down and Ren slows with me, sensing my dread. Am I ready for this? He's more than generous. More than accommodating, but he stops first and turns me to face him.

"Are you ready?" he rests his hands on my shoulders.

Before I can answer, footfalls on the soft ground behind us precede figures breaking the tree line. I gasp as Kaidin, of all people, has Jokinah bound and unconscious thrown over his shoulder. Renhin pulls me against him and I want to laugh. As if Kaidin has interest in me. Ren scowls as Kai pauses and looks down at me.

"Lendhi?" Kai keeps his eyes only on me. "Is this what you want?"

My answer catches in my throat. Ren's warm touch caresses my shoulders.

"Yes," I step back towards Ren. His arm comes around me. "This is what I want."

Kaidin doesn't want me as a mate, but it's

good of him to ask. I want to be in Ren's care now. He wants me. Kaidin is nice, but it's out of pity. I don't want pity.

"Are you sure?" Kai asks.

Renhin steps so he partially shields me from Kai.

"She's sure. Now fuck off."

"I didn't ask you," Kaidin's voice lowers.

Renhin tenses next to me and he reaches for his knife hidden beneath his skins. I hold my breath and press myself against Ren's warm golden skin, stilling his hand.

"I'm sure Kaidin, but thank you," my eyes flicker to Jokinah over Kaidin's shoulder. He wasn't gentle with her as Ren is with me. I wonder how well I really know him. His actions conflict with his words. I realize my foolishness. I only like what I imagine him to be. I don't know him anymore than I know Renhin.

Kaidin nods and stares at us. His blue eyes, a darker shade than Ren's, flicker between the two of us, standing in unity. He opens his mouth, but stops himself. He shakes his head and turns towards the village.

"If you're sure" he mutters over his shoulder.

Rustling from the brush snaps Ren's attention to the tree line as Yondin emerges. Bandaged and moving stiffly. I'm relieved he isn't dead. For a moment I forget the man I clutch is responsible for the wound. Dread and uncertainty drop a boulder in my stomach.

Yondin keeps his gaze down and away from us. Renhin doesn't relax as his cousin comes within spear distance. Yondin passes by without a word and

Ren straightens up, gripping me in one arm, and his spear in the other hand.

The village stands not far from us, reminding me I won't return to my sister's home, but to his. Ren's. This is real. I glance up at Renhin as he watches the figures of Kaidin and Yondin grow small in the distance. He loosens his grip on me, but slides it down my arm to grip my hand. As though he fears I'll change my mind and run. I'm not even tempted. This is better for me and my sister. And her children. And my…I might…well, I won't think of that now.

I grit my teeth and circle my fingers around his. I make my decision. He made his. Now we both face reality. Together.

I wish Kaidin didn't see us together. I wonder if my choice disappoints him. He has no right to be. Any lingering feelings I have for him only protect my own wishes of his feelings. He feels nothing for me and wants to ensure I'll be happy. It's a part of our deal.

When they're out of sight, Ren and I begin walking hand in hand. I try to slip my grip from his as we grow nearer, but he keeps hold and pauses to scowl at me.

"What is it?"

I stammer, "I thought you don't want them to see…us….so…"

"So?"

"Some hunters don't like to show affection in public," I remember Pandin. He never kissed or hugged or held onto Mirana in front of others. He thought it weak.

Ren sighs and offers a smile, brushing hair back from my face to hook behind my ear. He raises my hand to kiss the palm.

"Only weak men care about such appearances. Your opinion matters to me more than theirs. You're who I go home to. Not them. They are not who I have to worry about keeping happy."

I nod with a smile and replace my fingers around his.

"The elders and Perst won't think it strange I care for my hutmate. Will they?"

I shake my head. He knows what to say to me. He knows me better than I thought.

Drums of ceremony echo through the village before we reach it. The setting sun shines brilliantly on the huts and longhouses. No one pays mind to us as they focus on Kaidin and Jokinah's ceremony at the village center. When they are done, Renhin and I will have ours. My hand grows sweaty in his, but Ren tightens his hold on me and offers a smile as we approach the gathering crowd. My future hutmate stands more than a head taller than the villagers since most of the other hunters are gone, working. Only women and children and elderly are left behind during the day. A few hunters stay behind to guard the village from wild animals and raids, but they can't leave their posts.

The elders and Perst stand in a semicircle around Kaidin who looms over his prize. She's awake, bound and wide-eyed. Her chest heaves.

Pity pulls the corners of my mouth down into a frown. I remember her love for Ankhi, who stands on the edge of the crowd watching, her eyes glassy. Tears spill down her cheeks. Jokinah's own family is missing. I don't blame them. I don't want to watch this either, but the rest of the village does, eagerly.

The elders walk around them in a circle, creating a path with their footprints, while Perst chants. She talks of old ways. Bonding. Sacrifice. Of the Seer's first chosen children. Adamin and Evendhi. Mating ensures our tribe's survival. Our culture. Our people. We need more warriors to match the numbers of tribes across the waves. Another raid can come any time, but they always say that.

The elders sprinkle oil and bright red powder made from crushed petals over Jokinah, laying at Kai's feet, as Perst's voice raises in a crescendo. They shower Kai with it next. The drums stop. Silence settles before Kaidin squats down to grip his prize and hoist her over his shoulder.

I glance at the mating hut, their destination. After every ceremony the couple goes inside to mate while the village listens. To ensure their consummation. It might not be the first time, but it must be done for the ceremony. I skipped Mirana's ceremony. I didn't want to see or hear it. I spent the night at Banki's and Pandin came to claim me the very next day.

Mirana says the mating hut is nice. The furs and hides are new and soft. The beds have a bamboo frame and you never feel the hardness of the earth. It smells nice and has a tub of water only for bathing. Not washing or cooking. They leave you a small feast. Mirana says she could have stayed there forever, but then again she didn't want to be stuck in there with Pandin either.

Kaidin ducks under the hut entrance and Perst follows them inside with helpers. After a few moments Perst exits, closing the hide flap and securing it. A door isn't used because the village needs to hear the intimate sounds clearly.

Everyone listens with bated breath. I know what comes, as I have seen other ceremonies, but still I flinch when Jokinah cries out. The village cheers as her desperate yelps erupt from the hut. I cover my ears and close my eyes. I can't listen to this.

Renhin's warm arm slides over my shoulders and he pulls me against him. He leans over me, protectively. He kisses the top of my head, covering my hand with his over my ear, and it muffles cheering villagers. They wait until Jokinah quiets, but they are far too loud for too long. I bury my face against Renhin, willing him to shield me from this. I can't believe I hoped that would be me in there with Kaidin. But it will be. With Renhin. Perhaps not quite like that. I hope.

Whooping and hollering settle down to a lull of conversation and I dare a peek. All eyes are on us. I lower my hands and swallow the lump in my throat as I meet the eyes of the Perst. No more sound comes from the mating hut.

"Normally, the hut is awarded all night, but if there's a waiting pair we must proceed," elder Undel says. She smiles at us. "You finally return Renhin. Your mate seems willing."

Her faded blue eyes flicker down to our joined hands. Perst smiles.

Renhin doesn't smile, but pride coats his voice, "She is, grandmother."

I suck in a breath. I forgot about their relation.

Perst bows her head to us and the elders smile. Some of the other villagers do as well. They watch us without hunger in their eyes. They're soft and smiling, parting for us as Renhin guides me to the circle, the very center of the village. The helpers of Perst and the elders sweep away previous signs of Kai's ceremony, making it clean for us. Renhin sets down his pack and weapons before helping me with mine. My breath quickens and tears brim my eyes.

I'm scared.

I scan the crowd for my sister, but of course she isn't here. She doesn't know we're here. She's at home trying to scrounge together dinner for her runts. I don't want her here for this anyway.

Ren takes my hand and we walk to the center of the circle. The elders take their places and Perst hers. Kaidin drags Jokinah from the mating hut before we begin. His blue eyes find me instantly and he pauses before they disappear into the darkening village, unnoticed by anyone else.

Renhin turns me to face him, his hand on my cheek, and Perst begins her chant. I take a deep breath and go to my knees, readying myself to lie at his feet as is custom. Renhin stops me and pulls me up. He hooks his arms under my knees and shoulders to hold me against his broad chest. My eyes widen and in the crowd hands go up to open mouths. All of the elders smile past their work. Perst's chant doesn't falter, but she smiles wide. This doesn't happen. Ever. A catch is supposed to lie at her hunter's feet to show her subservience to her new hutmate.

Surprise washes over the younger generations while older villages cheer in elation. Renhin watches only me with a slight smile. He shrugs when my eyes meet his.

The elders circle us with Perst's chant wishing us good fortune. The same chant sung for everyone, but as I focus on Ren her voice fades. He leans in and nuzzles me. A laugh bubbles up from within and I squirm in his grasp. He kisses me and I don't notice the oil and red powder until it coats us. Renhin carries me over to the mating hut and through the doorway. The helpers change out the furs and hides on the bed. Food lies in wait on the table, steam rising from the fresh contents. Warm water sits in the tub, its own steam rising to mix with the food. Renhin holds onto me as the Perst follows us in. We wait in silence until the helpers leave.

"Go with the Seer's blessing and may He provide you with strong children. May He always keep their bellies full and their futures bright," Perst smiles, patting my hand. She waves a simple gesture of blessing over us before exiting the hut.

Renhin lays me down on the bed and oh, Seer, Mirana's right. So soft. I moan and writhe on the blankets as Ren sits on the edge of the bed. I freeze, aware the whole village listens to our every move. Ren smiles and leans over, dropping for his lips to meet mine. My nerves bundle in my stomach.

"I don't want them to hear," I whisper.

Renhin reaches up to the ties keeping my top together and pauses, waiting for my nod, before he pulls them loose. I bite my lip, blushing as he pulls my skirt away, tossing it to the fur covered floor.

"Don't think about them," he cups my breast with his large hand. I suck in my breath. "Just look at me."

His other hand slides up my calves to my knee before slipping between my thighs to open them.

"Don't look," I resist in the soft candlelight. He cups me and presses his fingers down between my folds. His fingers come away slick. He sucks them into his mouth and I shudder.

"You're beautiful," he pushes on my shoulder so I lay down. He picks up my legs and slides down until my thighs rest on his shoulders. I sit up, covering myself with my hands. His face is too close. He kisses my fingers, glancing up at me.

"I…I…Are you sure?" I know at some point I must pleasure him with my mouth. It's expected, but I've not heard of it the other way around.

"Yes," he smiles, kissing my fingers again. I hesitate before slowly sliding my hands up to my abdomen. "I told you this time will be different."

His hands curl over my upper thighs, widening me to him, anchoring me in place. I lay back, covering my face, unable to watch.

His warm tongue presses against my slick heat. Delicate. Violent pleasure shoots up my spine. I hiss and moan, arching my back. My hand cards into his thick hair as his tongue delves deeper. His hands slide to spread my lips for him. He sucks on my nub and I forget everything else. The villagers listening to my cries of delight. Kaidin. My sister. Everything. I can only focus on fire building within. Concentrate on how close I am to a squeeze. Washing over the edge as I do.

I lay back, limp, and breathe as Renhin slides up my body, kissing every inch he passes. I pay no mind to the taste as his tongue slides over mine. He grinds his hips. Far too much deer hide in the way. He reaches between us to loosen his wrap and I stop him. He pauses, studying me. I roll him over onto his back, and undress him. My gaze slides down from his glazed eyes to his hardened girth.

Growing up in Banki's hut, I know how this is supposed to be done. It's the right thing to do. My confidence shakes like my hands as I lean in and slither my tongue out to taste the glistening tip. He sits up on his elbows, brushing my hair away from my face before carding his fingers into it.

"You don't have to," he's breathless. The most vulnerable I've seen him. Now I'm certain I should do this.

"I want to," I lean over to take him into my mouth. His flesh is salty. Hard and covered in the soft silk of his skin. Loose and moving with my lips and fist that follows. I'm careful, slow. I don't think I'm good at this, but his moans encourage me and I find courage to take more of him.

He grips my hair and pulls me away.

"Come," his hand loosens from my hair. "Get on my lap."

I crawl up his body and he sits up. His large hands grip my hips, keeping them over his. The muscles in his arms bulge as he whispers, "Guide me."

I take hold of him, my shyness dissipating with each beat of my lusting heart, and he lowers me down over him. The stretch is satisfying. Sore muscles between my legs ache, but soon I bounce over him. Seer, I can't help it. His hands grip my ass, helping me into a steady rhythm. I lean against him, my breasts pressing into his chest, crying out against his neck and he moans. Relaxing his head back and closing his eyes.

We take it slow, drawing it out. So many times I almost squeeze before we pause to kiss and catch our breath. We restart again. And again. And again. I yelp with each bounce, with each breath, until my muscles spasm and he jerks into me, spilling his warmth into my body. Seer, I love this.

Sharing our breath, we pant and kiss, his hands rubbing up and down my back slick with sweat. They slide over my thighs before gripping and kneading my hips. Only now, coming off of my high, do I notice cheers of the village surrounding us.

YEAR ONE

Jokinah and I are the last catches, not surprisingly since the average Hunt lasts little more than a week, so Ren and I stay overnight. Renhin is anxious to get back to hunting. He wants to build up our stock before the dry months. He also fears a raid will come soon. He tells me his concerns as we walk through the village towards my new home. His hut stands in the newer part of the village, furthest from the shore and more inland. Better protected from raids and storms. There is space between the larger homes for room to grow.

I stare. It's large. Sturdy. Not crumbling mud and palm leaves like Pandin's hut, but hard clay brick and bamboo. The brick are smooth and stuck together with uncooked clay. The roof is wood from bamboo stalk. Windows have bamboo coverings. It's impressive.

Renhin smiles, watching me study our home, and shoulders both our packs, at his insistence. We press the wooden door open. When we enter, the first thing I notice is there are rooms. As in multiple. More than one. A great room with a fire pit dug out beneath the opening in the roof for smoke to rise greets us. Above the opening in the ceiling is a topper to keep out rain. Cooking and cleaning areas are close to the fire. A wooden tub is tucked into the corner. We walk into one of the rooms and I gasp, seeing a bed similar to that of the mating hut. Ren chuckles and sets our sacks down on it.

"You've been busy," I say, taking in the fine furs and skins. He built this place himself, perhaps with help, but mostly alone. As is custom.

One of Mirana's decorative baskets holds tools for skinning and tanning tucked into a corner. My heart aches at the familiar sight. I need to talk to her today.

"I prepared many years for this moment," his eyes follow mine to the basket. "I don't know if you remember, but I bought that from you. Sunspins ago."

"I do," I bite my lip. "I do remember that."

His grin widens. I blush.

I sit on the bed, my head light. New fears spring. Instead of being stuck with him, for now I find myself quite happy, I'm afraid I can't live up to what he thinks I can be.

"Can I go see my sister?" I ask, breathless.

"Of course. You don't need my permission," he sits next to me. "When I'm away I don't expect you to hole yourself up in here all the time. You need sunlight. Family."

I smile and lean into his offered kiss.

"Thank you," I whisper against his lips.

"For what?" he leans in to kiss me again. And

again.

He wraps me in his embrace. In heat and breathy whispers we attach. And I squeeze again. And again.

"Lendhi!" Mirana sprints from her hut, baby in her arms, and tears in her eyes. "You're back. Oh Seer, Lendhi, who got you?"

She stops short of me, kicking up sand of the worn trail from our hut, or her hut, to the village. I pull her into an embrace, careful of my nephew, who already cries and reaches out to me. We both cry with him and hold each other. She's warm and soft. And beautiful.

She parts us and uses her free hand to turn my face every which way to examine me.

"Who got you? It hasn't been a year," she glances over my shoulder, looking for a hunter, but Ren isn't here.

"Renhin," I watch her reaction.

At first, nothing. Her eyes widen and her mouth drops open.

"Oh no," she glances around as she lowers her voice. "How awful."

I smile and shake my head, taking her hand in mine.

"No, listen, Rana. He's actually…" I bite my lip. "Quite wonderful."

She leans back, cocking her brow, readjusting my nephew in her arms.

"Listen to yourself," she whispers. "You said

never. Never him. You hate him."

"But did I?" I ask. "I didn't even know him. Now I do."

She scoffs and guides me towards her hut.

"Let's get inside. The kids miss you. We'll talk in there."

I balk as we enter my old home. After the luxury of Ren's, I'm glad I won't return here. The darkness I once found soothing from the hot sun now suffocates. Packed sand floors, though swept clean of debris, cling in a powdery film to my feet. Grime presses between my toes. Already I miss the soft furs and wood flooring of my new home. Mirana has the skins piled in a corner, where they'll stay until time for bed. I won't miss sleeping here. Or eating here. Or doing anything here. I don't want my sister here either.

"He agreed to help us out. Help you out. I didn't even ask. He offered."

Mirana pauses and sets the baby down in a crude cradle Pandin carved out of salvaged wood that washed up on shore. My niece and other nephew squeal as they launch themselves at me. I wrap them in my arms, taking in their grubby faces, thin skins, and empty bellies.

"Remember what Pandin said? If it seems too good to be true, it is?"

"What did Pandin know? Mirana, Ren prepared for this for some time. He picked me out years ago. I came willingly with him. He's not what we thought he was. He's not what any of us thought. Just like you and I aren't what the village thinks."

"He's an asshole," she frowns. "He mocked Pandin every time they crossed paths."

I roll my eyes, "Mirana, *you*, mocked Pandin every time his back turned. I think everyone did. You just got unlucky—"

"Don't remind me," she watches her children as they release me to play. She sighs, "He's handsome at least."

I blush.

"He is," I agree with perhaps a little too much enthusiasm.

Mirana frowns in the dark before laughing.

"Renhin, huh? Who knew?"

We have room, and with a little convincing on my part, Ren agrees to move my family in with us. Because it makes me happy. I give him my thanks that night. Many times. And the next day. He skips a day of hunting so I can continue.

Weeks pass quickly and I'm busy. Settling in. Myself and the others. Helping with food and cleaning. Tanning and sewing. Gathering extra for market. Mirana continues her basket making and the children help at Ren's insistence. He says there's no such thing as too young to help. I agree.

At first, I ignore my missed courses. Then sickness. I can't ignore that. I hide it well, going out to the stream straight away in the morning. I don't say anything to anyone. Especially Ren. If I say it out loud it'll be real. I don't want that. Not yet.

Reality doesn't care about what I want.

With dry season approaching I try to wear modest skins in hopes of hiding the hardening of my abdomen. It's difficult with the heat, but works for a time. I know eventually, as Renhin worships my body on a daily basis, he'll notice it. Soon.

At the stream, as we wash the children, I tell Mirana first. Alone.

"I'm…I," I choke on the words.

Mirana pauses, swats her son's bare butt, and he giggles, running to join his siblings splashing in the stream.

She brings her dark eyes down to my hand resting over my stomach, "You caught child?"

"I think so," I swallow. "What do I do?"

She takes my hand in hers. She's warm. As always.

"Because our mother is gone, you must go see his. She'll take you to the healer of her choice."

I nod. I never bothered to learn these things growing up. I assumed to be an exception to their teachings.

"When?" I breathe out.

"Now. The sooner you see the healer, the better. You can start taking proper care. You don't want…" she never finishes, but I know what she means. I don't want to lose it. Like she did. The only time Pandin cried. That bastard. He was the cause of it and he had the audacity to blame it on my sister. It's always the woman's fault, even if the hunter hits her.

"Okay," my eyes follow the children around the bubbling stream and Mirana releases me.

"I've got the kids," she smiles. "Go ahead."

My stomach lurches as I stand, resting my hand over it. It's not the sickness of a caught child this time, but nerves. Renhin's parents are important people in the village. I never knew because I never cared to learn the hierarchy except for the elders and Perst. As the child of an elder, Ren's father is important. And his wife. I met them once, after my reunion with Mirana. A brief meeting, they were pleasant. I'm afraid I can't deliver their high expectations. Delivery. A baby. Me. A mother.

I press my hand against my mouth as tunnel vision brings me to their hut. His parents live close. Eyes follow me and I straighten up, trying to walk normally. I can't have rumors telling my hutmate I'm unwell. Already many catches from the Hunt have round bellies, but a few don't. Even those taken on the first day. I should be happy I caught a baby, but it terrifies me.

I face the bamboo wood door of their massive hut. They extended it over the years. Much like Renhin plans to do. They have a helper, a poor girl with no family rescued from Banki's hut, who answers the door when I knock.

"Oh," she ducks her head in a bow. "I'll let them know you're here. Please come in." She gestures inside and I drag myself into their great room. I think I know luxury from Ren's work until I set foot in this place. Foreign to me, I hesitate as the helper insists I sit in a chair shaped from bamboo stalks and covered in soft furs. The fire pit in the middle of the room lies unlit, as they have many fire pits throughout the house, and I stare into charred remains of last night's fire as I wait.

"Lendhi?" Ren's mother's lilt calls to me as she enters. "Hello child. Is something the matter?"

Renhin's father is where he got his height and strength, but his eyes and hair came from his beautiful mother, Tannah.

I choke before I can speak and her brows furrow. I stand as she approaches and pulls me into an embrace. She's warm. Kind. Maybe like my own mother was, if I could remember her.

"What is it?" she pulls away to study my face. "Is it Ren?"

I shake my head and blurt out, "I caught a child."

She gasps and hugs me tight. Clutching me to her before releasing to sweep my loose dark hair from my face.

"Thank the Seer," she smiles. "That's wonderful, Lendhi." She places her hand over my hardened abdomen. "Come." She takes my hand and guides me out of the house. Down the street and into the village.

"I haven't told him yet," I stumble after her.

"Good," she takes me through the cluster of huts closer to the oldest part of the village. "Never tell your hutmate unless you're sure. And you can't be sure until you see a healer."

She stops and faces me. Tears rim her eyes before falling down her cheeks flushed red from our walk.

"I'm honored you came to me with this news," she embraces me. I stumble into it. "I know I must guide you in your mother's absence and I cannot be happier. Don't hesitate to ask me anything."

"Thank you," I manage. I have Mirana, but perhaps I should include Tannah too. "I'm afraid."

She nods, smoothing my hair, "It's normal." She takes hold of my hand, and we walk.

I don't know why she keeps a grip on me; I'm

not going to run. Instead I tread after as my heart rises into my throat. Once I see a healer, it will be real. I wipe my hand down my face. I remember helping Mirana with her children. Her pain. Pandin's elderly aunt and Banki were the only women in town willing to help us without pay. So much blood. So much screaming.

Bile rises up in the back of my throat and I swallow it down as we approach a hut. Long and low, a giant building I pass many times and never give a second thought to. Sturdier, its mud bricks repaired often and thatch roof replaced with bamboo, it's known as the healer hut. Where healers of the village, always women, live and service those of us who seek, and can afford, their care. I've never been to a healer.

Outside, I read the short pictures of writ-speak carved at eye level by the door letting me know where I am.

We enter and the hut deceives us. It's deep and long. No one greets us, but Tannah calls out.

A woman no older than Tannah appears from behind a curtain hanging in a doorway on the wall in front of us with a smile. She's well fed. Her hides are new. Bright colored trinkets like Tannah's adorn her.

"Erdin, Lendhi needs checked," she leans in to whisper. "For child."

"Oh," the healer claps her hands together and gestures for us to follow her through the curtain of colored animal teeth to the back.

I attempt to get my bearings as we turn corners and duck through doorways, but give up as she guides us into a small room.

"I'll return," Erdin disappears, letting another curtain of teeth fall after her.

Tannah helps me to sit on a high bamboo bed in the center of the room. She holds my hand, standing next to me.

"There's not much to it," she pats my hand. "You'll drink a brew."

"That's all?" the smallness of my voice startles me.

"Yes," she smiles. "It tastes awful, but that's all."

I nod, certain I've tasted worse. Rotten fish out of desperation. Sea slugs. Other things one must eat to survive. I paid the price afterwards sometimes, but she doesn't need to know that. Those days are over for me.

Erdin returns with the promised brew steaming in a clay mug. I take the offering and drink it. I grimace, pretending it's worse than it really is.

Both women watch me in silence. Their gazes pierce as I deflate beneath them. Tannah keeps hold of my hand, which begins to sweat. My stomach gurgles. I already lost my breakfast earlier today. I flush as I cup my hand over my stomach.

They chuckle and exchange a smile.

"That's normal," Erdin croons. "We'll give you some things to help with sickness and discomfort. Plus a brew to drink every morning with breakfast to ensure your baby's growth."

I nod and smile. That seems to be the response that pleases everyone. My sister. Tannah. Everyone, but Ren. He can always see through it.

Sweat breaks out over my forehead and I need air. I bend over, slipping my hand from Tannah's and hug myself.

"Lendhi," Erdin croons again, as though to a

child. "Look at me."

When I drag my gaze up, Tannah bursts into tears. My eyes widen and she embraces me, again.

"Congratulations Lendhi, you are with child," Erdin turns her back to me. "I will return."

Tannah laughs and wipes her cheeks, "I'm sorry. I'm so happy. What a blessing. To start a family so soon."

I offer another quiet smile and Erdin returns with a woven basket full of bottles. She points to each one, telling me when to take it and how much. What to mix with water and what not to. What foods I should avoid. What activities to avoid. I will need to return in a moonspin for her to ensure everything is all right. And every moonspin after until the baby comes.

Tears brim my eyes, "I'll never remember all of this."

Erdin smiles and I want to slap it off of her. She pulls a piece of vellum from the basket, "It's all in writ-speak right here for you."

Mirana didn't have this. These brews and instructions. She took care and ate what she could when she could. Her babies are fine and healthy. What do I know though? I sigh and Tannah takes the basket for me, insisting she carry it.

Tannah asks Erdin for a calculation of conception. Heat flushes my face as Erdin thinks.

"This is soon, so at the ceremony I think."

It could have been in the days leading up to our ceremony, but this pleases Tannah.

"A sign from the Seer, surely," she says.

Tannah takes me home to find Mirana with her runts and they exchange a polite greeting. The children bow to her as Renhin taught them. For a moment I allow myself the fantasy of how my hutmate will be as a father. He's good to my sister's runts.

Tannah sets down the basket and Mirana rifles through it with her children, telling them to be careful. Tannah guides me to the room I share with her son. She closes the door and sets me down on the bed.

"Zerendin will be ecstatic," she coaxes me to lie down. My hutmate's father is hard to read. I can't imagine any emotion from him, but perhaps this will be an exception.

My eyes grow heavy and I don't hear her leave the room.

I pace in our great room. Alone. Mirana takes her brood into their shared room.

Fire burns bright and high in our pit to combat the growing cold outside as the sun dips down to the underworld.

I want to get this over with. Telling him. And get this all over with in general. But to what end? I'm expected to do this more than once, but I'll cross that bridge when I get to it.

The door opens and I whirl round as Ren carries in field dressed animals. He goes in and out, making many trips, and when I offer to help him he refuses. He unties his cloak from his broad shoulders and his lips are cold when he leans over to kiss me. Without thinking I attend to his bounty. Then I remember I have something to tell him.

He pours the water I have heating over the fire into our tub to wash grime and blood. He strips, glancing at my sister's closed door, and gets in. He sighs and relaxes, sinking. The water clouds with dirt and blood. I stand, blood on my own hands, and approach the tub. I wash them in the water and Ren raises his brows.

"Something the matter?" his blue gaze penetrates mine.

I take a shuddering breath, trying not to cry. He sits up, the water sloshing, and reaches for me, his wet hand gripping my forearm.

"What happened? Something happened. What is it?"

I can't find words and tears spill down my cheeks.

"Len, tell me. I'll kill them. I will kill them, Lendhi. Tell me what happened," his blue eyes light up, reflecting the fire burning close to us and within himself. He starts to raise from the water, but I stay him.

I slide his hand from my forearm to place it over my hardened abdomen. He stills.

"Child," I bite my lip.

His scowl softens into a broad smile.

He pulls me down into the water to sit in his lap. I yelp and laugh. Water splashes onto the furs around us. His arms crush me to him and his warm lips cover mine.

My belly swells. Too much. Too soon. Tears streak down my cheeks as Renhin argues with his father over the life growing inside me. Zerendin stands from the dinner table laid out with a feast Tannah took hours to prepare and points his accusing finger at me.

"You mated with another before Ren found you," he knocks a basket of bread off the table. Tannah cries out and reaches to still him and he slaps her hand away. "You weren't pure."

Renhin, his face red, stands, knocking his chair back.

"Don't," he points at his father. "Don't. You don't know what you speak of."

"I know precisely what I speak of," Zerendin rounds the table to come towards me. Renhin places himself between us. "When a man lays with a wo—"

"Enough," Ren places his hand on his father's chest to stay him. "Not another word. She was pure when I took her. And even if she wasn't, I don't care. I. Don't. Care. She's mine."

I huddle down into my chair, hoping to be forgotten. I can't help a sob as they continue to argue and scream at each other. Tannah's eyes meet mine over the forgotten food. She shakes her head, tears brimming her blue eyes, and reaches out to me. I grip her hand.

Ren silences his father with a push. The older man stays on his feet. My hutmate didn't try very hard, but his mouth gapes.

"Come, Len," Ren pulls my cloak from the back of my chair and wraps me up in it before he gets his.

We leave their house without a word.

"I'm sorry," he puts his arm around me. Rain pours outside and I huddle against him. "I'm so sorry Lendhi. He'll see. Soon he'll see. I didn't know he was going to do that. You don't have to see him again. How do you feel?" He lowers his hand to my protruding womb. "How's our baby?"

My heart races in my chest and I wipe my eyes.

"I'm fine. We're fine. This is fine. We'll be fine."

He pulls me to a stop and turns me toward him.

"We are fine. More than fine. We're good. We're happy. Our baby will be happy. So what if he grows a little fast?" he smiles. "He's healthy."

"Ren, you know I didn't...I..."

He shakes his head and pulls the hood of my cloak further over my head to protect me from the rain.

"I know, Len. I was there," he smirks. "Don't worry about me. And as I said...I don't care either way."

I nod. His thumb brushes my wet cheeks and he leans in to kiss me. We walk hand in hand in the rain, our cloaks tight around our bodies, and get home. Mirana, who never gets an invitation to Zerendin's house, chases her children around the roaring fire in our great room. They laugh and giggle. She stops and pants.

"Back so soon?" she straightens up.

Renhin shrugs and goes to our room. My stomach rumbles and I grab one of Mirana's nicest baskets.

"I'm going to apologize to Tannah," I say to

Ren as he comes back in. "What happened is not her fault and she spent a lot of time on that food."

"I'll go with you," he reties his cloak.

Mirana cocks a brow, but doesn't ask. Her eyes follow us out of the hut.

I carry the basket, shielded by Ren from the worst of the wind and rain, and the helper lets us back into his parents hut. I follow Ren through the house and we stop when fervent talking erupts from the next room.

"She isn't the one," Zerendin says over Tannah's soft crying. "She's a waste."

Ren freezes and pulls me to the wall next to him.

"She's not a waste," Tannah sniffs. "How can you say something like that?"

"The only reason I set Ren on her to begin with is she's good breeding stock. My son will never make chief if he keeps raising other hunters' children. She's a soiled catch. She belongs in Banki's hut, not in our son's home. I never should have told him to take her. We should have gone with someone else. Now he'll be forced to take a second hutmate. I must convince him to cast her out."

"Zeren," Tannah cries out, anger consuming her grief. "Don't you dare."

I cover my mouth and watch as panic settles over Ren's face. His eyes wide, he shakes his head.

"No," he reaches out for me, but I slip away. His hand snaps out to grab my wrist. Our eyes meet.

He doesn't want me after all. He never did. Why is he pulling me to him? I wriggle free and, holding my stomach, race out.

"Len!" he calls after me. I push past the

helper out into the cold darkness. I run without reason, supporting my extended womb, until nausea forces me to slow down to a walk, turning every which way. Ren finds me, in minutes, but what else can I expect from a hunter like him? He's gentle as he pulls me into his warm embrace.

"Let me explain," he shouts over the wind. Flurries of rain in the high wind beat against us. My teeth chatter and he shields me, pulling me over close to the nearest hut. The rumble of his chest vibrates against my ear as he talks.

"At first it was an order. A long time ago. More than five spins around the sun. He picked you."

I jerk to get away, but he holds me to him.

"I fell in love with you."

I hold my breath.

"When I bought that basket from you…that's when it started. I thought you weren't good enough for me. Until then."

Burying my face against his chest, I snake my arms around him. He tightens his grip, careful of my stomach.

"I watched you. Learned everything I could about you. I knew I had to have you. Whether my father wanted it or not. All that time before we came back. In the wild. On the plains. When I talked to you, that was me. I wanted you to want me. I wanted you to come with me. I have loved you from afar for so long I didn't want to ruin it. I didn't want to start off that way. I didn't want to force you or make you unhappy, but I couldn't let anyone else have you. I didn't know what I was going to do if you said no. I thank the Seer every day that you said yes."

I stop chattering as he warms me. My eyes

close and I lean into him.

"I love you now. And I will love you always."

My heart stops before pounding in my chest, fighting my ribcage containing it. He loves me.

"I...I love you too, Ren," I whisper against his chest. Wind and rain drown out my voice and he turns away, taking my hand.

He guides me back to our hut. I let him help me until we cross our threshold. Mirana throws a glare at Ren when she sees my face. She stands and I shake my head at her. Instead, she takes her children to their room.

Ren takes care to untie my cloak and sits me on our bed before pulling my hides off. He dries me with a clean fur and sits down, rubbing his large hands up and down my legs. Warm, I relax and close my eyes, relishing his gentle touch.

According to the healer, I'm three-quarters to maturation, but already I tire easily. My womb is so big and that's part of the problem.

Ren watches me, silent, his hands working warmth back into me.

"I was supposed to stay away from you. That's when I bought the basket. I was curious."

My gaze slides to the basket in the corner. I use it all the time and never noticed how faded the color is. Quite old indeed, but taken care of. Treasured.

"When we talked, you lit up. You smiled," he has one of his own as he talks. "I think it was that singular moment."

"Why didn't you say anything before?" I sit up on my elbows. "Why did your father pick me? And for what?"

Ren sighs and lays me back down before spooning me from behind. His warm breath tickles the back of my neck. His fingers run along my arms.

"What could I say? You didn't even seem to like me. We hardly spoke. How could I say something without sounding insane?"

True.

"My father wants me to be chief. Chiefs in the past always had one mate. The argument is, if you're too busy running things you don't have time for more than one woman. You come from a fertile, but poor, family. A family incapable of fighting back if…if there was a problem. He picked you for this very thing."

His hand slides down over mine on my swollen womb.

"I just want to be with you," he inhales, burying his face in my hair. "I make love to you even now because I enjoy my time with you. I don't touch you just to plant a child. I touch you because I want to be close to you. I can do that as chief, or not. I don't care."

I settle down into his warmth, and the fur blankets.

"I'm happy, Ren," I breathe out. "You make me happy. I know I misjudged you for a long time. And as someone who hates that, I shouldn't have been that way." I roll over onto my back and look up at him.

My lips freeze a moment before I blurt, "I love you too."

He kisses me, "You don't have to. I'm content you don't run away."

"No," I run my hand through his golden hair. "I can't imagine running away from you."

He smiles.

"Why do you need to become chief?" I ask.

We settle down under the sealskin blanket and face each other. I tuck my face up into his neck.

"You know the old ones?" his hand runs through my hair. "Who walk and never die?"

I stiffen. Of course I do. They're the ones who drove our people to the islands in the giant whale. To get away. Sometimes I have nightmares they rise out of the oceans and eat us all.

"Yes," I press myself against him.

"Before their time there were more tribes and villages. Everyone spoke differently. The heads of these tribes were preserdents."

I nod against him.

"They held a lot of power," his warm hand rubs my lower back and I refrain from moaning. "As do the chiefs, but you can't conquer another tribe or village without a chief. My father wants to be chief, but he's too old. He wants me to do it and for us to take over other islands."

I pull from him and look up into his blue eyes.

"What? He wants you to go to war? Us?"

Ren sighs and brushes my cheek, "Yes."

"No," I squeeze him. "Please, no."

"Don't worry about it now Len," he lays on his back. I rest my cheek on his warm chest. "Get some sleep. Our son needs it too."

I lay awake all night. Thinking of Ren's father. How horrible the man is. His poor mother. And war. No, I don't sleep at all.

109

I hate it when Ren stops speaking to his father.

It's because of me. I want them to get along. I tell Ren how lucky he is to have his father at all, but he doesn't listen. He won't talk to him because Zerendin insists I mated with another. Ren can't convince him otherwise. I don't step foot in their house again. And neither does Renhin.

Tannah comes to visit, ever supportive, and insists on being here for me. I love her for it. Her husband doesn't grief her for this, since he says it's in her nature. This helps Tannah and Mirana bond and they become fast friends.

Moonspins pass and warmth puts me in better spirits.

I can hardly walk. Erdin says I have one moonspin to go before I can expect to labor. As it draws near my anxiety grows. My baby moves a lot. Mirana's runts sit around me and feel my swollen stomach, laughing and giggling. Singing to it. Trying to play with it while my poor sister picks up some of my slack. The children help her. Renhin does too, but he focuses on hunting more than ever. I worry about him. I feel so useless.

I lay in bed, woken by pain. I try to roll over and fall back asleep against Ren's warmth. He nuzzles me in his sleep and pulls me closer. I cry out and sit up. Pain shoots through my lower back and I pant when warmth spreads out from between my legs. Ren sits up, his eyes bleary.

"Len?"

"Baby," I swing my legs over the edge of the bed.

Ren jumps to his feet and fetches a deerskin cloak for me. He calls for Mirana who appears in the doorway.

"Baby," he helps me to my feet. She disappears.

Another pain hits and I clench my teeth. It almost brings me to my knees, but Ren keeps me up. Sucking in air I try to curl in on myself, but I can't. Oh Seer, this is it. I can't focus. Fear and pain cloud any thought process. Ren lifts me into his arms. Summer heat and spice scented air waft into the hut when Mirana opens the door. She disappears from sight. I cry out again, clutching my stomach. The baby moves. He's ready. So am I.

Ren tells me it's all right. I'll be okay as he carries me through the village. I don't feel like that's the case as he carries me past familiar bead curtains of colored teeth. He lays me out on something soft and I cry out for him when he leaves my sight. Tannah and Erdin crouch close, Mirana with them. Warm hands hold mine. They help me step over a hole in the ground lined with soft furs. I squat over it. Covered in sweat, I cry out until my voice is hoarse and my throat raw.

"Beautiful girl," Tannah rubs her hand over my back. "You're doing so well."

Pain.

It starts again. And again with increasing

frequency. This is the worst. I can't do this. I change my mind. I want to jump up and go back to how I was. But I can't. Time blurs. Pain is everything. I push and excruciating agony as my baby slips free. Erdin's waiting hands catch it and she pulls a wriggling baby from beneath me. She turns it over, slapping its back. It screams. I pant. Gasp. Breathe. I smile as she wraps it up.

"A boy," the healer smiles.

Tannah cries out, rubbing my back. They support me as I stand, but additional pain stops me. I cry out and squat again. Erdin frowns and sets my baby down in a cradle.

She crouches down before me again, "We're not done."

"What?" Mirana shrieks. Her grip tightens. "What did you say?"

Tannah keeps hold of me. She rubs circles over my back before running her fingers through my hair.

"You did so well, but a little more," she coaxes. "Just a little more."

I shake my head, "No. Please." I can't do this. I'm so tired. Again I push past pain when they tell me. Erdin keeps her hands beneath me and catches another baby. She swaddles it in her own cloak, not prepared for two, and slaps its back. It joins its screaming brother.

"Another boy," Erdin smiles, laying them side by side.

Tannah laughs.

"More," I gasp. "More." I know it's there. It's coming. How? Am I being punished? Has the Seer finally forsaken me? Is he punishing me for Pandin's death?

"It's the after flow," Erdin rearranges the cradle for two babies.

I shake my head. Crying I turn to Mirana. She nods and lets me go. I push again and she catches another baby. Dear Seer. Three. Three babies.

Tannah cries out again, keeping me from collapse.

Erdin takes my third baby from my sister. I fall against Tannah, knocking her back. My third baby screams to life.

Burrowed beneath blankets, I can't move.

My three boys lay in three cradles stuffed into the small birthing room of the healer's hut. Mirana didn't have it this good. She didn't have the luxury or support, but in my defense she didn't have all three of her children at once either. My boys are so small, but Erdin insists they're healthy. Very healthy.

Now they sleep, but I can't. I stare at them. Marveling at their scrunched faces. Serene closed eyes. Two of them have wisps of blonde hair. The third raven black. I watch them wriggle around in their wraps and coo in their slumber. I smile at them. I love them.

The door opens and Ren slips in. He kneels next to me, pulling my hand from the blanket, and kisses the palm.

"Len," he brushes my cheek. "My beautiful Len. You did it."

I smile at him and curl my legs tighter. He

rubs my cheek with his thumb, laying his chin on his arm on the bed. We stare into each other's eyes for a long time before he turns to the cradles.

He stands, watching them. He dares a soft touch. To one's cheek, another's blonde hair, and the last's curled fingers.

I relax into the furs. Knowing he's here, watching over me, I can sleep.

The sun dipped down into the underworld hours ago.

I want to go to bed, but instead I sit in our great room holding Devrin, my firstborn, in my lap as he suckles my breast. Zerendin kneels before me, his forehead on the fur carpet at my feet. Mirana holds Calidin and Tannah cradles Vandin in her arms. Once, before their falling out, Ren might have named one of our sons after his father, but not now. I want to scold the old hunter. Tell him he's the fool, not my hutmate. Instead, I take a deep breath and reach for kindness.

Undel, one of the elders and Ren's grandmother, stands behind Zerendin. Her eyes shine in the firelight. This apology is her idea.

"My son learns humility," she wrests her gnarled hand on Zerendin's shoulder. "As have I."

My eyes widen as she makes to get to her knees, but Ren steps out from behind me and stops her.

I don't know what to say, but I do have the pride of knowing I hold up my end of any deal ever made in my relationship with Ren. Their expectations are met. In excess.

"I…" I know I should say something smart. Smooth things over. I struggle.

"I don't know what you're talking about," I smile. "What is there to have humility for?"

I want them both to grovel a little more. To be so burdened by guilt they stoop. Undel already stoops, but it won't hurt her face to drag the ground. Especially now I know she's the one who insisted I carried another hunter's baby. I won't be fooled by her fake smiles again.

Undel nods with a smile. Insincere. She pats Ren's forearm and sees herself out of our hut. Tannah's cold gaze follows the old woman. There must be history between them. Zerendin sits up on his haunches, keeping his eyes down.

"I will redeem myself," his eyes meet mine. "I'll learn not to reach hasty conclusions." His gaze slides to Tannah next to me. This apology is to her as much as to me, "Please, forgive me."

I clear my throat, "There is nothing to forgive."

Ren smiles.

But really, I want to punch Zerendin in the throat.

Morning sunlight shines down on us as we wash the children in the stream. It's difficult, near impossible, to carry my boys alone. Tannah spends everyday with us, helping not only with her grandchildren, but Mirana's runts as well. Ren's mother is in heaven. Having been able to only carry Ren, after many failed attempts, children surround her. We all smile and laugh as we watch her chase my nephew through the water. He laughs, running on sturdy, chubby legs. I thank the Seer Ren can provide for such a big family.

Screams erupt from the village and I jump to my feet, Calidin in my arms. Something comes. We bundle the babies into slings, one for each of us, taking the hands of Mirana's children and we leave with caution. The older children know to be quiet. We tell them of raids all the time. And the clang of weapons, banging of drums, and destruction of doors and windows being smashed in tells it is a raid. Cries of anger and desperation carry past.

We skirt around the village, keeping out of sight in the brush, until we reach our hut. Once inside we shut the door and pull a wood beam over it. We shutter the windows and bar them. We crowd into the room I share with Ren and lay the babies down in their cradles. We cover them, singing softly, trying to keep it quiet and dark. But for a few croons, thank the Seer, they're quiet. My heart thuds in my chest. I have survived raids. We all have, but each one can be the last. Or the one where they drag us away to another island. As slaves or sacrifices.

I pull a spear out from beneath the bed. Tannah and Mirana tuck the older children into a corner and cover them with a fur blanket. I ready myself, standing at the door. Of the three of us, only I can brandish a weapon. Only I have used one. But Seer, not on a human.

My palms sweat. I wipe my brow. Heat stifles

us without a breeze blowing through the windows.

A thump. Close. It's the door. I tremble and scowl.

The last raid was when I was seventeen spins around the sun. They attacked the village in the cover of night. Pandin stood before us. His large belly hung low over his waist, but his hands were strong. It was the only time in my life I had faith in him. Prayed for him to stay alive and protect us. The only time I needed him to be strong. Pandin was bad enough to deal with, but he was an evil I knew. Knew how to handle. I didn't want to be free of him to endure a worse fate. I made ready, in case he fell, with my sister and her runts crying behind me. The raiders overlooked us. Much to Pandin's, and our, embarrassment, the raiders thought our hut abandoned. Or at least, that's what the other hunters said.

Another thump and cracking wood jerks me to the present. I stare at the closed door to our room. I widen my feet. When the wood splinters, the door bursting open with a kick from the other side, I cry out and lunge. The warrior, covered in red war paint, yelps and twists his torso. My spear end slices his side, but doesn't penetrate. He grabs my spear and yanks on it. I stumble forward, refusing to let go, and he drags me out of the room. The children, my babies, cry as another warrior darkens the doorway to our hut. I yank my spear from his sweaty grip and brandish it.

"Oh, ho ho ho," the second warrior laughs and jumps back. "Oh, I want her."

"I saw her first," the first lays his hand over his wound. It comes away coated in blood.

I bare my teeth as their eyes focus on the dark room behind me.

"Are those your babies?" the second looms close.

My chest heaves and I back away, trying to watch them both at once.

They share features, from the same father perhaps? Their hair slicked back stays out of their faces. Their war paint in hand prints over their torsos and jaw. One stands taller than the other, but both are similarly built to Ren. And intimidating, like Ren. And I don't give a shit.

"Fuck off," I lunge with my spear. They jump back again. "Go somewhere else."

"Yeah," the first grimaces. Blood runs down his sweaty ribcage. "Those are her kids."

They split, each circling a different way.

"We need breeding females, sweetheart. I'm afraid we need *you*," the first snatches out, grabbing my spear.

I roar and yank, throwing him off balance, sending him into the dying embers of our fire pit. He cries out and jumps free, dancing around.

His partner laughs, before striking. Quick. Agile. I'm no match for his speed or strength. Or experience. He wrestles the spear from my hands and throws it to the wall. The head embeds in the brick. He pins my arms to my sides and I kick. So hard. So. Hard.

Mirana cries out and launches herself from the room. Tannah stays with the children, shielding them.

The first warrior, his feet cool, grabs Mirana's wrist and she spins. He removes a weighted strip of leather from his belt and hits her over the head with it. He catches her as she slumps. He hoists her over his shoulder.

"I got mine," he mutters, leaving me to the mercy of the second.

Still in the grip of the second warrior, I kick and scream and thrash. The first warrior lays Mirana down at his feet before stepping over her. He approaches me, my captor turning me to face him, and hits me over the head. Pain explodes behind my eyes and I slump, moaning. I blink, forcing my eyes to focus as the second warrior slings me over his shoulder. I catch sight of the first warrior staring at Tannah in the doorway. She glares at him.

"My son will kill you," her cold voice carries through the children's crying. "He'll find you and he'll kill you."

"I'm sure he will lady," my captor says over his shoulder.

He carries me out into the bright midday sun. The world spins. I cough, bile rising in the back of my throat. Chaos reigns in the village. Screaming. Fires. Smoke. I can only look on helplessly as an invader rapes a woman on the street. I reach out to her before falling limp against my captor.

Panic electrifies my limbs to life and I kick when the waves of ocean drown out the voices of raiders. Gulls cry out overhead. I scream, creating a chorus with other hostages. Those who aren't gagged. My captor flops me down onto the sand and presses his foot on my chest. Fast movement spins the world around me and I grasp his ankle, but I lack the strength or orientation to do anything else.

"Gods, you're tough," he smiles down at me.

"Can't even knock you out." He shouts overhead, "I need a rope." He kneels down over me and binds my wrists and ankles on the wet sand. He laughs, stuffing a piece of tough hide between my lips. I scream past it, hoping he sets fire of his own accord. Why isn't the Seer helping me? Us?

The warrior lifts me over his shoulder and steps into a longboat. He sets me down at his feet while he sits on a benched side. Others are here. Mirana lies unconscious on the other end. The boat pushes off shore and other raiders hop in. It rocks as they take paddles and fight the waves. They laugh and joke.

My captor doesn't paddle, but lays back. He watches me and I can't tear my gaze away from him. If I didn't hate him with every fiber of my being I might think him handsome beneath the running paint. He leans over me, rubbing his hands around my head, and I wince when his fingers press against the raised bump where his brother struck me.

"I'm going to give you my seed," he speaks over the waves and men. "And you're going to give me babies. Like those back there."

I shake my head.

"Oh yeah," he grips my upper arms, pulling me close. I strain against him. "I'm going to ride you again and again and again. I'm Arde, and you'll scream my name by the end of the night."

Tears spill down my cheeks and he smiles, sitting up.

Horns blow in the distance and my captor swivels in his seat. He stands, the muscles in his legs bunch as he keeps his balance. He shouts orders for the rowers to quicken. They speed up, pumping. Our own longboats pursue with hunters aboard. Renhin stands at the front of the first one. I launch myself up towards my captor and knock him off the boat. He falls out, sputtering and splashing. The rowers stop and other raiders get to their feet. They refuse to leave my captor. He's significant.

I fall against the seat, my head swimming. Arde's hand clutches the edge of the boat and climbs in with help. He kicks my stomach, spitting on me before picking me up and hauling me to my feet. I dangle in his grip.

"Fine," his hot breath smells of alcohol. "Go back to your man. I'll come for you later."

I laugh before he throws me over into the water. Salt water stings the wound on my head. I sink, trying to kick my bound legs. Trying to swing my bound wrists. I can't hold my breath as long with a gag. Water seeps into my mouth and down my throat. Into my nostrils. I swallow uncontrollably. My chest bursts and I focus on the sunlight above rather than the dark waiting below.

A splash above and hands grip my wrists, yanking me upward to break the surface. I gasp and retch water past the leather in my mouth. Renhin holds me; he yanks the leather from my mouth, slapping my back, helping me breathe. Oh Seer, he has me. The longboat he rode glides by, catching up to the enemy. Ren pulls his hidden knife and cuts the ties at my wrists and ankles. I clutch him as he treads water, his arm around my waist.

"Len," he kisses the crown of my head. "I've got you."

I relax in his grip. Another of our longboats passes by and he takes hold, dragging us behind. His arm bulges as he pushes me up into it. Hands grip my arms and haul me in. Ren follows after, lifting himself from the water. Kaidin's worried face hovers over me.

"Lendhi?" he runs his hands up and down my arms. "Are you all right?"

Renhin shoulders him away with a glare, "She's fine. Paddle."

Kaidin frowns, glancing at me before he takes hold of a paddle. Renhin sets me down at his feet, between his knees and I hug myself, shivering in the warm sun. The cold water stole my warmth. I imagine Arde, the kidnapper, fulfilling his promise. Hovering over me. Sweating. Pressing into me. Hurting me. I can't shake it. My hands curl around Renhin's leg. He looks down at me, but picks up a paddle to help. They're trying to catch the others. Trying to get the other women back. Mirana.

I sit up.

I take an empty seat and unstrap another paddle from the boat floor. Gritting my teeth, I dip the paddle into the water. I have no experience with this, but I have to do something. Many stare, including Ren, but no one complains. No one dare says a word.

I bite my lip, fighting the burning muscles in my arms as we catch up. The first longboat in our train rams into their last. The one with Mirana. With Arde. While our longboat passes the first, Renhin jumps up, knife in his mouth, and launches himself onto the other boat. I paddle, watching over my shoulder as long as I can. He'll be all right.

He'll be all right.

We take some prisoners. We kill a few.

Some of the boats get away. Not all of the women taken were Hunt age and their fathers do all they can to keep from weeping. Hunters who lost their mates pace in anger and curse and yell at each other. They ask questions. Why didn't we leave more hunters to protect the village? Why don't we have better alarms in place? Raiders never took this many before. Never took this many women. They take food. Goods. Rarely slaves. Something's changed.

I huddle against Ren, his arm around my shoulders and thumb rubbing my upper arm. He holds me tight. I can't get away from him—not that I want to. I cling. My pride went down in the water with me. I want him to hold me and he does as we sit, watching the other hunters argue. Kaidin has Jokinah. He rescued her from another boat. Mirana remains unconscious, lying at our feet, covered in Ren's sealskin cloak. Erdin examined her first. The healer kneels over one of our hunters with a fresh cut on his arm. Other healers from the big hut tend to the wounded. For a price.

I study Kaidin with Jokinah. They're not intimate. They don't hold each other. They speak, calmly, but with no affection. Not all couples have it. I suppose I'm not surprised. Jokinah loves Ankhi. Jokinah's belly sticks out and I try not to think of Kai forcing himself on her. Or her forcing herself to please him. Theirs must be an unhappy pairing either way. They both deserve better. At least, she does.

I suck in a shuddering breath and Ren plants a

kiss to my temple. His father steps up into the midst of the argument, quieting the growing crowd. The whole village is here to see what happens. Who returns. Who is lost.

"If we have a chief we can solve these problems."

Ren tenses beside me. He's not ready for this. Neither am I.

"The elders can never agree," Zerendin gestures to the huddled figures. "And our Perst has no say in war. A chief can get things done." He doesn't need to say who should be chief. We all know who he's thinking of.

"In the meantime," Zerendin stalks over to the prisoners grouped together. "We have their chief's son." His crocodile smile doesn't fool me as he looks down on the warrior who took me. The enemy's hate filled eyes focus on me. Narrowing. Ren bristles next to me and stands, letting me go. I shiver without his warmth. I lean over to brush Mirana's hair from her forehead.

Renhin brandishes his spear and holds the tip at the man's throat.

"Don't, look, at her," Ren's soft voice carries over the wind.

"I'll do more than look," Arde keeps his eyes on me past Ren.

Ren balls his hand into a fist and strikes the warrior's jaw. He drops his spear to withdraw his knife and it stops just short of Arde's throat when two hunters grab Ren's arms. They pull him back. Ren frees himself and paces.

The hunters argue more. Long into the night, but they take it to the longhouse with the elders and

Perst. I take my sister and myself, when she wakes, back to our hut. We find Tannah there with the children. None of our things are gone, but many are broken. Women were the prize today. Tannah cries and hugs us when we fill the doorway. I embrace her before pulling away to check on my babies. They sleep in their cradles. Mirana's runts sleep in a pile on the bed. I touch each of their chubby cheeks. Ensuring they're here and real and all right. I sigh.

I leave the sleeping babes and join Tannah and my sister in the great room. We sit by the fire as Tannah tends to Mirana's head, applying a paste of herbs to it. The herbs Ren put over mine dry and his mother sings to us softly and coaxes my nerves by running her hands through my hair. I fall asleep next to the warmth of the fire.

I wake alone on the floor of the great room to Ren curling up behind me, encasing me with his arms and his legs tangle in mine. I still and think. How fast time goes. How fast our babies grow. How much my hutmate makes love to me. How he loves me at all.

I hug his arm to my chest and he stirs. He nuzzles my hair and plants a kiss behind my ear.

"Len," he whispers.

"Mm?" I roll onto my back to look at him.

He grips me and kisses me.

"It's done," he cups my cheek.

My heart ignites to life, thudding against my aching head.

"You're chief," I bite my lip. He nods.

YEAR TWO

In the beginning, change is subtle.

Already they treat me different. Better than I have ever been treated by the village. People come by asking if I need help with the children. Or cooking or cleaning. People whose names I don't know. I refuse them all, content to keep it to Mirana, Tannah, and myself. As it has always been.

A ceremony takes place before Ren can take his as chief.

Everyone gathers in the village center at sunset. Even those who live past our village borders in the wild. Everyone on the island. Everyone.

I'm one of many in the crowd as Ren sits in an ancient wooden chair. He wears a sealskin wrap with fine detailed bone I sewed on and war paints of black and white over his torso, back, and arms. His blonde hair is slicked back with seal oil so the headdress of bone and paint and feathers can sit atop the crown of his head. His blue eyes are cold as he looks above our heads, somewhere in the distance.

He's mean. He looks how I used to think of him. Distant. Cruel. Uncaring. But I know tonight he'll take me in his arms and warm right up.

The elders, including his grandmother, chant around him under Perst's guidance. The helpers of our religious head bring out the chest with the shiny bone piece. We wait in silence as they open it and the Perst withdraws it. They attach it to her ceremonial spear and she dips it down into the flames of an open fire close by. Renhin kneels down from his seat and she comes round. He balls his hands into fists, bracing himself. I chew my bottom lip, gripping Vandin. Devrin sleeps in a sling hanging from my shoulders against my back and Tannah holds Calidin. Mirana is busy keeping her runts in check.

Perst presses the hot shiny bone, glowing with heat, between Ren's shoulder blades, but he doesn't cry out. He sweats, shakes, clenches sand between his fists, but never cries out. He will serve as chief until he dies. It is likely our son, Devrin, will take his place.

The village kneels as Ren stands. The elderly. The pregnant. It doesn't matter. Perst gets to one knee, holding onto the ceremonial spear. We grovel on the ground before our new ruler, keeping our eyes down. I dare a glance up and catch Ren's eyes on me. I offer him a smile and see a flicker of one from him before I cast my gaze back down. Like I should.

Our titles change first.

Now I am to call him husband as he is more than my hutmate. I am more than his. He is to call me wife. We are the only two people in the village to have these titles until Ren can no longer reign.

The second to change is our residence.

The stone house of past chieftains opens after two generations. They repair and clean it up. We have many helpers and hunters who are called guards. The house is made of stone taken from the mountain. Large. With more than one layer. I'm sad to leave our family home. A home I think luxurious and fine. A home I'm ready to die in.

I stand on an outcropping of the stone house they call a balcony. From this height there's a view of the entire village. Helpers build up a frame for our new bed out of stone behind me and fit it with the finest furs and hides the village has to offer. They guarantee it rivals the mating hut in comfort. I balance Vandin on my hip and brush my fingers through his thick dark hair. He smiles at me, toothless, sitting up on his own, and places the flat of his palm on my cheek.

"Bu bub u buuu," he laughs and I do too.

Ren stands behind me. He holds Devrin and leans over to kiss me and Vandin on top of our heads.

"Are you ready for this?" I turn to face him.

"I'm ready," he inhales my scent, nuzzling my hair. "To have you."

I giggle as goosebumps coat my skin.

"Are you ready?" he cups my cheek.

"No," I shake my head, nuzzling his palm. "I've never been ready for any of this."

He nods and rests his large hand on my shoulder.

"You're perfect, Len. Keep doing what you're doing."

I shrug, "And now you can't hunt?"

He shakes his head, "I can sometimes, but village business is considered more important. Now all huts will donate their best meats and furs to us so I can serve without distraction."

My mouth quirks.

"What if someone can't?"

"I won't tell anyone if you won't," he smiles.

I return it and cup Devrin's chubby cheek. He smiles at me and leans into it as I run my hand up to mess up his blonde locks. Vandin whines in my ear and I turn to kiss his forehead.

"You're going to get out of practice and fat," I scrunch up my face.

Renhin laughs.

"Never," his smile remains. "I have a sparring partner. He'll keep me in shape and on my toes. I'll still protect you. With my life."

He sobers and sighs.

I study his face.

"That chief's son, Arde," I watch as helpers come in and out to set up our things. "Is he still giving you trouble?"

"He knows how to get to me," Ren readjusts our son in his grip. "That's all. I should be more careful of showing my emotions."

I want to laugh. My hutmate...husband, doesn't show his emotions often. Not outside of our room, but I understand. I want to know what the warrior says and does, but I don't either. I don't want to know what fantasies this Arde cooks up while locked in our cave of punishment. A place far from our village dug into the side of Wailing Cliff.

"What are you going to do?" I ask.

"Trade. Him and the other prisoners for our women."

I nod, "They must miss their hunters."

I watch my children in both our grasps. Hoping someday someone doesn't decide to keep them locked up for ransom. I like to think my sons won't capture slaves with intentions of rape, but I'm sure Arde's mother thinks this of him as well.

"We sent out someone with a message to meet on the center isle and make our exchange."

My heart thuds in my chest, "I don't want you to go."

The center isle is neutral territory laying between large islands belonging to tribes in the ocean. I've not been, but know of its use. In the past it held a market for trade and getting together, when all the tribes got along. As time passed we became enemies. Now the center isle is only for use in battle or negotiating. Far away. I don't like it.

"I have to," he sighs and brushes hair back behind my ear. "This is who I am now. I must go."

"Then don't be chief," tears cloud my vision. "Take it back."

His warm lips meet my forehead and his breath ghosts over my skin, "You know I can't."

Later in the night Ren pushes into the heat between my legs and I arch my back as he moves over me. My cries echo against the stone walls and I bite my lip, but he drags it out of me. And by the end of it, after his seed warms my womb, we sweat and pant. I'm warm in his arms.

Our messenger returns after many weeks.

It's Yondin. He comes to us in our great house after the sun disappears into the underworld. He holds out a piece of vellum with writ-speak on it. Renhin reads and throws it into our burning fire of the great room. Dry months fast approach and gales of wind push against our closed bamboo shutters.

Kaidin joins us not long after Yondin's arrival, along with others.

My heart aches. It's been so long since I've seen him. Or Jokinah. They have a daughter now. I can't help wondering if she might be a match for one of my sons. More than joy for Kaidin, I pity Jokinah. A daughter isn't what she wants, but we none of us are guaranteed a son anyway. I wonder if my parents were disappointed I was born a girl. It's stupid. Without girls none of us would be here.

"What did they say?" Ren paces.

I lean against a post in the shadows and Kaidin's eyes find me and he nods. I return the gesture. Crossing my arms and kicking up my leg.

I shouldn't be here, but I don't care. Neither does Ren.

"They agree to a peaceful trade," Yondin drinks our fruit juice and water and eats our cooked meat. I stop the helper at the door with another plate for him and take it in myself.

Yondin looks up at me and offers a crooked smile before taking the plate.

I sit by the fire and watch my husband pace. Kaidin watches me. Yondin watches all of us.

"I told them what good care we take of the chief's son, Arde."

"I don't care," Ren stills. "When do we meet?"

Yondin finishes off the juice, tipping his head back for the last sweet drops to slide down.

"Three weeks," he wipes his mouth.

Ren crosses his arms and nods. Kaidin watches everyone in silence.

My abdomen grows again. I go with Tannah to the healer.

Erdin congratulates me on another child caught. I'm happy to have another child with Ren. Fear and dread aren't even a thought as we walk back to our stone house with a light step.

Ren meets us with guards.

"We're leaving," his hand brushes my cheek. "It's time."

The guards and Tannah distance themselves from us.

Tears spring to my eyes, "But Ren, I'm with child again."

"Len," Ren whispers as he leans down to kiss me. "That's wonderful."

I slide his hand from cupping my cheek down to my womb. He rests it there, warm against my bare skin. I close my eyes. He kisses my closed lids and brushes my wet cheeks with his thumb. I hold his hand against my abdomen.

"Don't go," I open my eyes. "Please, don't go."

Ren sighs and hooks my loose hair behind my ear.

"I have to. You know that. I'll be back soon."

Kaidin and Yondin stand amongst the hunters and guards joining him. My eyes meet Kai's and he steps up, staying behind Ren.

"I'll be with him," Kai smiles at me.

Ren tenses and keeps his blue eyes on me.

I nod. This brings me comfort. I pull Ren down to kiss me again before he passes by, the men following. Some of the hunters go. Others stay. They disappear down the way before Tannah lays her hand on my shoulder. We walk back to the house with my guard.

When the sun rises later, I know something's wrong.

The exchange should be over by now. It's been almost a week. The passage of time confirms my worst fears. I retch in a room we use for relieving, sheltering from the cold morning and prying eyes. I hate this part of pregnancy, but it must be done to get to the rest.

Commotion breaks out downstairs and the door to my room bursts open. Soft steps approach the closed door next to me and I gasp when Kaidin swings it open.

I hold my hand over my mouth.

Blood covers him. His wounds are shallow, but many. He pants and kneels before me, pulling me against him. Dried blood flakes between us and I start to cry. I circle my arms around him. Sliding into his lap, our hips cradle, and he runs his large hands down my hair to rest on my back.

"It's Ren," he whispers against my forehead. "He's dead."

I wail into Kaidin's warm embrace.

Zerendin calls a meeting of the elders and Perst with other prominent village members in our house. Members who will be called elder in the future.

I don't care.

Tannah and I weep as they talk about war and vengeance. As they remind us the enemy took Ren's body as a trophy. Kaidin was one of many who witnessed them drag my poor husband away. They must have vengeance. Those that lived were lucky to get away at all.

I don't care.

Tears flow until none are left. I hold my son, Devrin, the new chief, in my arms as the men rile themselves up. Kaidin watches me. His dark blue gaze peers past the light of our fire in the great room.

Still, I don't care.

I look down on my son and see his father. My stomach aches. I cup my hand over my hardened abdomen. This baby will be my last.

Tannah and I are honored to be the only women at the war council who have no title or place in village hierarchy, but as Ren's mother and wife.

I don't care.

Zerendin gestures to me, "Look at her."

I sob and cover my mouth as Devrin fusses. I don't want them to look at me, but he goes on.

"Remember her face. His grieving wife. Pregnant. Holding the future of our village in her arms." He speaks of avenging his son with no emotion. He tries to use my sadness to compensate for his lack thereof.

The men mutter in agreement. Kaidin remains silent.

"We go to war," Zerendin holds up his fist and the other men shout in agreement. The elders nod their heads, faces grim. Perst remains quiet. Unmoving. She has no say.

I. Don't. Care.

Yondin betrayed us. That's what happened. He made a deal with the other tribe to hand over Ren. Revenge for the Hunt. It doesn't matter to me. It's done now. Yondin isn't here, so I cannot run him through. All I can do is grieve the love of my life.

Zerendin comes round to talk to me alone in our great room. I hold onto my oldest son. I have to be with him always. He's the spitting image of his father. I can look into Ren's eyes when I look at Devrin.

"Your place is safe, Lendhi," Zerendin rests his hand on my shoulder. I shrug him off. "You can stay here and raise your sons. The future chief," he reaches out and I pull Devrin away from his touch. "Should be with his mother."

I scowl and meet his eyes, "Was that ever a question? Of course he'll be with me."

"Of course," he smiles. It never reaches his eyes, and he doesn't answer me. "In the mean time, Tannah and I will live with you and your sister. Until Devrin is of age to become chief in truth."

Sighing, I push Devrin's blonde hair back from his forehead. He sounds out words. Saying Mama. Tears well my eyes. Over time I know he'll forget his father and I worry I will too. Will Ren's face grow to a fuzzy, distant memory like my parents and brothers? I sniff and nod.

"Of course," I clear my throat. "I trust everything to your care."

Zerendin smiles. Now it reaches his eyes. This is what he wants. Himself in charge.

After weeks of preparation, the men of our village have their war. The other tribe waits for it, but we triumph. They sing Kaidin's praises, especially, at our victory celebration. Or so I hear. I don't go, sitting alone in the stone house with the children and Mirana. Grief winds around my heart and crushes it in the rhythm of the drums. I remain immobile. Singing and cheers lilt over the crickets in the brush. Everyone but me forgets the man who died. The hole in our lives. Maybe it's just in mine.

Kaidin becomes the next chief. The elders and Perst agree, this is the right step. Zerendin is furious, but Kaidin's prowess on the battlefield and strategic leadership impresses them. They think it best a grown man takes over. Better than my infant son who has many years to grow. I agree with them. We are at war with a tribe for the first time in generations, and not having a chief is weakness. We need leadership. We need a chief. It pleases me to see it taken from Zerendin. Everyone knows he would lead through my son. Now he is nothing. It's the least he deserves.

Kaidin's ceremony mimics Ren's. I attend with my family. Jokinah stands with her head high, her daughter on her hip. My heart seizes. I don't think about her. Or anyone. I hope she finds happiness. I hope she and Ankhi slip away together sometimes. I hope for their love. I remember mine and when my tear glazed eyes look up, I find Kaidin staring at me.

Mirana and I pack our things, with help, to empty the stone house for Kaidin and his family. I have charge of the children while Mirana and Tannah place our belongings into wicker baskets upstairs. Since Ren left us, we don't have much. It's better this way.

I chase after my nephew, catching him, and he giggles, kicking his feet, when Zerendin darkens the doorway of the great room. I stop, panting, and set my nephew down. My three sons crawl around in their pen built from bamboo. A gift from one of the village families after Ren's death.

I swallow and walk over to the pen, resting my hand on the edge.

"Your sister isn't coming with us," Zerendin scowls. He isn't happy. And unappreciative of the kindness Kaidin shows us by allowing time to leave. The old hunter is more angry about losing power than his son.

My heart drops into my stomach, "She must."

"No," he holds up his hand. "As head of your hut I say so. I can provide for you, and my grandchildren, but I have no obligation to her and hers."

I shake my head, glaring, "She comes with us. They all do."

"You can either leave her, or we will leave you and take the children. Ren's son will be chief someday."

My babies watch us in silence. Mirana's runts do too. All eyes are on me. My mouth hangs open as I think. I turn to him.

"Then we will leave. You are not the hunter of our hut. You cannot take my sons from me. That is law. I will live with my sister in the house Ren built."

Zerendin huffs, "You're a bigger fool than I thought." He turns from me, his hope for my ignorance dashed.

My heart thunders in my chest. My hands

shake and sweat.

Zerendin tries to take them, but the elders, Perst, and Kaidin, side with me. They order Zerendin to either take my sister and her children, or none of us. Tannah pleads with him, but he turns us out. No one in the village will speak with him now.

The hut Ren built stands sturdy, but empty. In the time it went unoccupied it fell into some disrepair, but still it fairs better than some. Like Pandin's.

I step into musty darkness and my lips tremble. I want my Ren back. I can't look at any part of the great room without a memory or tears filling my vision. Mirana thinks I should leave her and stay with Zerendin and Tannah, but I can't. She's all I have.

We spend our first week making minor repairs, what we can, and living off of what food we have left. I take most of our valuables to market to trade for food, but soon the house empties of all but the most basic essentials. It's empty. In more than one way. I try to scavenge and fish like I used to, but there are almost twice as many mouths to feed now. Without proper hunting, providing for six children and two adults, me being pregnant, is too much. Even with helpful baskets of extra food left by strangers in the night. Seer bless them. Mirana makes her baskets and her daughter helps. She's old enough. Ren taught her children to work and work they do. What little they can.

Tannah sneaks us food and skins when she can. Once she comes to us with a fresh bruise welling on her face. We don't ask. She doesn't tell. Instead, I hug her in thanks.

I grow large. My sons grow fast, but not fast enough. Panic sets in nightly. I can't birth in the comfort of Erdin's hut again. Our hut is clean, and we do what we can, but I'm afraid. So afraid.

The sealskin cloak Ren gave me during the Hunt wears thin. I wrap it close to my rounded body as I stand knee deep in cold morning water to scavenge mussels and other food. Sea slugs. I pause. Before the Hunt I had hope. So full and bright and beautiful. After the Hunt I relished in happiness and comfort. Now there's nothing. Despair. Worry. I contemplate sending my boys to live with Zerendin after all. Though Mirana and I starve ourselves for the comfort of the children, it will reach an end. Villagers will stop giving us their food. Someday Zerendin might keep Tannah from coming. We survive only on the kindness of strangers and my stubbornness.

The surf crashes against rocks and I keep a grip on my basket, crying. I don't know what to do. I'm hungry. I'm tired. Miserable. My baby kicks against me and I cry out, leaning against the rock, catching my breath.

I pull myself together, as I do so many times a day, and round the rock, bumping into Kaidin who keeps me on my feet.

I mutter an apology and straighten up, but he doesn't release his grip.

"Lendhi," he guides me from the water and

takes off his own sealskin cloak. New and warm, he pulls it around my shoulders. He rubs his large, warm, hands up and down my arms.

"Kai," I swallow. I'm not done crying and my face twists in concentration as I try not to. "How kind of you. What are you doing here?"

He slides one of his hands to cup my wet cheek. His thumb wipes beneath my eye.

"Looking for you."

"Why?" my face crumples. "What do you want?"

He sighs and leads me away from the shore line. I support my extended stomach with my free hand as we make our way to the tree line. Goosebumps raise on his tan skin, but I don't offer his cloak back. I stare down at the near empty basket I clutch. He waits for my sobs to quiet before he speaks.

"I would ask how you are but," he regards me with furrowing brows.

I laugh before I start crying again.

"I never wanted any of this," I wipe my eyes. "I want Ren back. That's all I want. I want him back."

Kai presses down on my shoulders until I sit with him at the base of a palm tree. He pulls me into his warm embrace and lets me weep against his chest.

"I know," he mutters against my dirty, tangled hair. "I know you do."

I release him, shaking my head.

"What do you care? You have other things to worry about."

He sighs and takes my hand, gripping it tight. He won't let me pull away from him. He doesn't speak until I raise my eyes to meet his.

"You," his hand brushes my cheek. "I worry about you."

"I'm fine," comes the automatic response. To him. To Tannah. To Mirana. To everyone.

"No, you're not," he tucks his thumb to my chin as I turn away, forcing me to face him again. "You're skinny. You're filthy. Big with child. Ren would…turn in his grave seeing you like this."

Shame heats my face and new tears erupt from my eyes spilling down. Ren doesn't have a grave. They can't bring his body back for me. He lies out there. Somewhere. A rotting trophy. I'm so tired of crying.

"Well, he's not here, is he?" I want more than anything for what I say to be a lie.

"But I am," Kai holds my hand between his. "And I am chief now."

"I know," I bite my lip. "I'm sorry I spoke out of place."

He shakes his head, "No. That's not what I mean. You can talk to me however you like. As always."

I roll my eyes bringing a small smile to his face. I mirror it.

"Lendhi," he swallows. "I'm going to take you as my hutmate."

I stare at him. It's not a question. A statement. I chew on my bottom lip. All hunger and fatigue momentarily forgotten.

"What?" I whisper. "What did you say?"

Kaidin's hand slides behind my neck and he brings my face close to his. My heart thuds in my throat. Is he going to kiss me? I ball my hands into fists. I'm not ready for this.

"I'm taking you as my hutmate," his dark blue gaze stares into mine.

"I don't understand," I shake my head, brows furrowing. "Why?"

"I love you, Lendhi."

My baby kicks with the surge of my fluttering heartbeat. I smooth my hands over my stomach and heat rushes to my cheeks.

This is too little too late.

"I have always loved you," he continues, not letting me back away. "When I made that deal with you, I didn't want Jokinah. I wanted you. I made a deal with her to help me get you, actually. I wanted to take you both as my hutmates and she could be free with Ankhi, but you're the one I wanted. I still want you."

My mouth hangs slack as he speaks.

"I let you be with Ren because you were happy. He made you happy and that's all I wanted for you. But I can't stand seeing you like this. I can't. I can't sit by and watch you starve. I can't let you grow thin and tired. I know you're sad. I know it's too soon. You miss Ren, but come with me, Lendhi. Please. I'll take your sister. All of the children. There's more than enough to go around."

His hands grip mine, encasing me in his warmth. His own fluttering heartbeat pulses against my hands. Nervous? Is he anxious? Do I have a choice?

"I…" I swallow.

"I want you to bear my children."

I shake my head, "You have a daughter with Jokinah. If that's true—"

"Her choice. Her decision. I never forced her.

I only do as she asks. It was one time and at her insistence. Her and Ankhi see each other often. I don't care. When we're settled, Ankhi will move in as a helper so they can be together,"

"But what about you?" I look down at our joined hands.

"I have always wanted you, and only you, Lendhi."

My eyes snap up to his. I've heard this tune before. Renhin said the same thing. I don't doubt Ren's love for me, but Kaidin seems just as sincere. Is this why they always hated each other? Me? That's ridiculous. Stupid. Impossible.

Had I known. Had I known all along. How different things might be. I would have let Kaidin take me. I wouldn't have fought him at all. Not like I fought Ren in the beginning. Kaidin didn't have to convince me. Cajole me. He could have asked and I would have said yes. Without hesitation. But now I do hesitate. That's another life. Another time. Another Lendhi.

"I'm not asking," he breathes out a held breath. "I won't take no for an answer."

My brows furrow, "You'll force yourself on me?"

"No," he frowns. "Never. I want you safe. Fed. Comfortable."

I slip from his grip and rest my curled fist over my engorged breasts ready for my child to come soon.

"Lendhi," he snatches my hand back, pressing it against his chest. "You can lay with me if you want, but I still love you. I can't have you living like this anymore."

"And what will the elders say?" I shake my head. "Jokinah? You're trying to take a soiled woman as a hutmate."

His grip tightens over my fingers, "You're not soiled. You're a widow. You're Lendhi. Don't talk about yourself like a basket. If you came to me the day after your ceremony with Ren I would have taken you. I have never cared about the puritan bullshit Perst drones on and on about. Or village rumors. I never will. But also," he hesitates. "They already approve. Jokinah too."

I laugh, bitterly, "You sought their permission."

"Not exactly," he mutters. "I declared to them I'm taking you. If they don't like it then I'll resign as chief. Instead, they encourage me."

My brows raise.

"They think you'll be a good wife. As you have already proven. Jokinah is going to step down from that position," he sighs.

"What?" I rest my hand on my womb as my baby kicks again.

"You're quite popular with the village and elders. Even Perst likes you."

"Because they all know I can give you children," my voice is flat. "Obviously." I gesture to my extended stomach.

I allow myself a smile with him before it disappears. It feels strange to smile.

"I love Ren," I glance at my hand pressing against his chest. "But before him, I think I loved you."

He stares at me, his grip slacking and my hand slips from his.

145

"I wanted you to take me in the Hunt, but I thought you wanted Jokinah," I lower my gaze.

He grimaces and shakes his head, "I'm foolish. If I had been honest with you maybe we could have been together."

"No," I look back up at him. "I won't trade my time with Ren for anything in the world. Or my children."

He nods.

"But it's not hard for me to imagine," I inhale a cold shuddering breath, my cheeks taut with dry tears. "Being pleased as your hutmate."

He smiles and reaches out, his thumb rubbing my cheek.

"But I need time. I can't…I can't go a minute without thinking of Ren. I don't want to warm your bed with thoughts of Ren," I take hold of his wrist to pull it off.

His smile disappears, "Of course. I don't want you to either."

"And you'll care for my sister?" I hold his hand between mine. "Her runts?"

"I planned to," he says. "Even before the Hunt. I know how much they mean to you."

Ren did too. I nod, heart pounding. I don't want to betray Ren's memory. He hated Kaidin, but I don't want my children hungry. Or to be in Zerendin's care. I want my new baby healthy.

"And Jokinah? How does she feel?" I let his hand go.

"We discussed it. She doesn't want to be a wife. She's more than fine with you taking over that role. She just wants to be with Ankhi. In fact—" he inhales and shuts his mouth. "Never mind."

"What?" I ask.

"It's not important," he rubs the back of his neck.

"It is," I smile small. "What does she say?"

I fidget under the heat of his dark blue gaze, "She's disappointed in me for not fighting Ren for you to begin with. She thinks I'm weak."

I laugh, my eyes dropping to his muscular chest covered in war paint depicting his importance as chief. He smiles and shrugs.

"She does," he laughs with me.

We quiet. Sobering, I loosen his cloak from my shoulders, offering it back to him. He takes it, shakes his head, rewrapping it around my shoulders. He ties it and I bask in the thick warmth.

"I can't have you until your baby comes," he smooths the cloak down over my arms. "But I paid Erdin to help with your birthing. And to bring you some brews to start taking. You'll birth this baby as you did the others. Once that's done your family will join into mine."

I bite my bottom lip and nod.

"Until then," he continues. "I'm gifting you all you need. When is your birthing? Soon?"

I nod as he dares to rest his hand over my womb. My breath hitches and he removes it.

"Good," he says.

We part ways. I carry the near empty basket back to the hut. Mirana rests in the darkness of our hut, dirty and tired, cleaning a fish I caught this morning. We keep it shut up and dark when the weather is cool because wood to burn is hard to come by. We must save it for cooking and cooking only.

When I tell her the news, she smiles. Then

frowns.

"I can't keep living off of your kindness. I should be taking care of you, not the other way around."

I slip the new cloak from my slender shoulders and fold it. Ren's remains wrapped around me.

"You took care of me most of our lives. Shielded me from Pandin. Kept me housed and fed. This isn't a trade at market. We take care of each other," I offer a smile.

She returns it. We spend the rest of the night in silence.

As my boys slumber under the new warmth of Kai's cloak, I curl in on myself, as much as I can, and cry. I don't want to go to Kai. At one time I cared for him, but it's passed. Hasn't it? What was that flutter I felt when he touched me? Why aren't I repulsed? Why am I excited? I hate myself. I betray Ren with each weak thought. I didn't deserve Ren. Perhaps that's why he was taken from me.

Seer, I miss him.

I don't want Kai. I just want Ren back.

In the middle of the night my birthing comes.

Pain wakens me and Tannah, who stays with us now to help under Kai's orders, takes me to Erdin. We leave Mirana behind with the children. Word travels fast and Zerendin beats us to the healer's hut. He waits outside. I pause long enough to spit at him, my saliva landing at his feet. His face remains grim, but he steps back. Kaidin runs up to us from the darkness, panting, guards following. Zerendin's hatred seeps through his calm demeanor. They exchange a glance before Zerendin bows out and sets himself aside.

A wave of agony brings me to my knees and Kaidin snatches me from Tannah's grip, picking me up. I can't focus as he carries me into the hut, brushing past the familiar curtains. Erdin greets us, sleepy, but prepared as she guides us to the birthing room. Kaidin enters and sets me on my feet in time for a contraction to hit. I stagger to my knees and cry out, my hand on my stomach. He starts forward, but Erdin coaxes him back. Tannah helps me to my feet and guides me further into the familiar room.

This time is different. I know what to expect, what to do, but it doesn't lessen the pain. This baby is bigger than my sons were and I can feel it as I squat over the skins. Though more painful, the birthing is fast.

I lay in bed wrapped in warm hides with my new daughter. Tannah cries with me. We both think of Ren as we watch her sleeping. She looks like me, with dark eyes, but her hair is golden like his is. Was. I kiss her forehead as she wriggles in my arms. Tannah rests her hand on the crown of my head.

"I miss him," I sob. "I miss him so much."

Tannah shakes her head, leaning over to kiss my hair, her own tears flowing down her cheeks.

"I do too," she whispers, her warm breath

coating my hair and skin. "I do too."

I feel like we're the only ones.

Kaidin comes to call the day after. And I say no. I continue to resist him for days. I'm not ready yet.

I sit inside the great room of our hut next to a small fire bathing my newborn daughter. I named her Windhi, after my mother. She's the first child I get to name, as Ren named our sons, as is custom.

The sun shines high in the sky, covered by thick rain clouds. With windows shuttered and the door closed, inside our hut is dark and toasty from the fire. Lit by the generous wood Kaidin gave us. The children nap. Mirana and her eldest, her daughter, sit and work on baskets, keeping quiet. My baby is too young to giggle or play, but her dark eyes look up into mine. New and unfocused. I smile down at her, singing softly.

"Lendhi?" Kai calls from outside for the eighth day in a row.

Mirana pauses, her hands blue from berries she uses to dye the leaves. Her daughter's dark eyes land on the door. I follow her gaze. Rain and wind push against the wood, droplets of water blowing in from the gap beneath it. My heart pounds. I'm not ready to leave Ren yet. I'm not ready to leave the hut where we held our children together. Where we made them together. Where we lived together…I'm not ready.

I pick up my daughter and wrap her in the

seal cloak Kaidin gave me, drying her. I swaddle her and leave her by the fire. As I tuck her in, at a safe distance from the flames, pounding snaps my attention to the door.

Wood splinters as Kaidin kicks it open. He steps through, opening our hut to the elements. He wears layers of skins and furs, increasing the width of his shoulders. He looms over us, looking down, almost menacing in the light of our fire as shadows dance across his features. He gestures to someone outside.

My sons stir in their pen and my nephews rouse from their nap amongst old furs.

Guards follow Kaidin in and his eyes fall on me as I scowl. He waits, the firelight dancing in his eyes, silent as guards approach us with blankets and cloaks.

"Come," Kai holds out his hand.

I exchange a glance with Mirana. So much for a choice.

Kaidin's frame intimidates me in the layers of furs. His shoulders wide. He dwarfs the great room. I wonder what his hut looks like. Not the stone house, but the one he built, thinking I would live there. I wonder how it compares to Ren's.

"Lendhi," Kai's voice takes a commanding tone. He scowls. Heat rushes to my cheeks.

"Yes?" I muster as much innocence as I dare. "What is it my chief?"

Kai flinches at the word, but points down to the children, "Bundle them. Get their things."

The guards nod and I stay my protests on my tongue. I can't resist. We need his help. It isn't pride. This is betrayal. To Ren. Kaidin expects me to lay with him in the same place I did with Ren. The same room. Possibly the same bed. I don't know if I can. I don't know if I can give him what he wants. I'm afraid.

The guards are gentle with the confused children. Mirana wipes her hands clean and helps them. I pick up my baby and cradle her as I stand. Kaidin approaches and wraps another new sealskin cloak around my shoulders. He chafes my arms against the cold of the rainstorm. He wraps his arm around my shoulder and guides me out. I don't dare resist now. I glance back to ensure my sons, bundled against the rain, are taken care of.

I walk with Kaidin through the village. Others greet us as we pass with smiles and whispers. They, at least, seem happy with our union and follow us. Happier than I am. I try not to look too sober and return greetings with a nod. I clutch my little Windhi to my bosom. Kaidin stops in the village center, in front of the elder longhouse. Everyone gathers, despite the weather, and with great trepidation I realize, it's happening now. The ceremony must take place before I can live with him. Shame heats my cheeks. My tangled hair is pulled back from my face. Dirt runs in lines down my wet face from trudging around in rain. Tannah steps up, Zerendin in the back of the growing crowd, and she offers a smile. She rests her hand on my cheek before gently taking my baby. I won't give Windhi to anyone else right now. Not even Mirana, but with Tannah's unspoken blessing I feel better about what's to come.

Kaidin draws me into the circle. I kneel at his feet in the traditional way as the elders circle us, the Perst chanting. Rain pours down over us, washing away the circle of tracks the elders leave to ensure the longevity of our mating. Ren held me in sunshine. Kaidin keeps his hand on the crown of my hair, looking down at me, with perhaps affection. I can't tell. His eyes never leave mine, even when they sprinkle us with oil and red powder that runs in the rain. I stand with his assistance and the Perst follows us into the hut. It's prepared. They expected this. I did not. I wonder if they did this for eight days, waiting for me.

Perst finishes with the same speech I've heard before and leaves us alone. I glance at the bath and food. My heart thunders in my chest, matching the weather outside. I can almost feel the Seer's displeasure in the weather. I'm not ready for this either. Not yet.

Kaidin removes his layers of warmth until he's in his traditional chief's wrap and bare chest. Paint accentuates the muscles of his torso, though it's damp and runny. He sits on the bed, looking up at me.

I wring my hands.

"I'm not ready," I whisper, knowing they listen outside. I can't trust the pattering of rain to hide my secrets. "I can't do this."

"You don't have to," his voice is warm, like his eyes, in the dim light. "Bathe. Eat. Get comfortable. We're in no hurry. And we can…pretend."

"Pretend?" my eyes widen.

He nods and leans back on his hands, "Jokinah and I did on our ceremony night."

It brings an unexpected smile to my face. I'm glad he didn't force her after all.

"All right," I untie the cloak at my shoulders.

I entertain asking him to look away, but he turns from me already. He knows I don't want him to see me.

The warm room contrasts the howling wind and torrents of rain outside. Wet and cold can't penetrate the layers of protection the ceremonial hut offers. Steam rises from the bath water and I fantasize about cleanliness as I disrobe. My hides pile at my feet and I step into the water cloudy with soaps and herbs. I let out a held breath and relax.

Kaidin turns back to me, my body hidden by the water, and leans on his side. He watches me bathe in silence. I submerse myself and wash my hair. Once clean, I twirl my finger and he smiles before turning away. I stand, letting warm water run down my body. I take the fur from the table next to the bath and dry myself. I grimace as I pull my dirty hides back on. I run my fingers through my hair, sitting on the other side of the bed.

"Now," he turns back to me. "You need to cry out. Like…you're squeezing."

Heat flushes my face and chest, "I can manage that." I think.

I study the room, hesitating. The whole village listens. I don't know how to begin. Unaware of how I sound when Ren brings…brought me pleasure. I just do it. I look at Kaidin and shrug.

He frowns, "You don't have to pretend to enjoy it. Just that it's happening."

"Of course I should enjoy it," I say. His brows raise. "I mean, I don't…I—"

He raises his hand, "It's fine. Relax."

I straighten up and drag my gaze down to the floor. A deep throaty moan escapes my throat before I close my eyes and yelp. Loud. It's enough, as the cheer of the village beyond the hut's mud walls erupts.

Kaidin smiles.

I do not.

Kaidin shows great patience with me.

Jokinah welcomes us with warmth. Ankhi moves in soon and Kaidin sleeps alone as they lay together. I sleep with my sister in our shared room with the baby. Our children, accustomed to each other's company, are happy to have their own. The stone house has plenty of space for all of us, and we live as happily as we can. Kaidin takes care of village business. The elders and Perst are happy with him. The people are happy with him. We rally our defenses when threats face us. Yondin, now a prominent member of the enemy tribe, sends writ-speak personally to threaten Kaidin. And he mentions me by name, but Kai refuses to tell me what he says. The guard who said all this to me in passing has a bruise on his face the next day.

I feel guilty, but stay quiet. I won't make that mistake again. Neither will he, I suspect.

Dry months pass. Then wet. Now it's warm. Sunny. Flowers bloom in the brush. Our children totter around and Windhi kicks her legs as she crawls. We sit with guards down by the stream and the children play in the water. Trees shield us from the harsh rays of an afternoon sun. I keep Windhi on my cloak as she chases a jeweled beetle around it.

Kaidin sits, holding his daughter in his lap,

pointing to the trees. Showing her birds and naming them as he does. She smiles and basks under his attention. She has her mother's build, but her father's coloring. For a brief moment I allow myself to wonder what our children would look like. Will look like. Jokinah and Ankhi walk side-by-side down the stream. Guards watch us all. Mirana approaches, wet from playing with the boys, and sits next to me on the soft grass. It's a beautiful day.

I stop Windhi from teetering off the cloak and set her back down. I pick up the little beetle and place it before her. She laughs and follows it clumsily. I smile.

"You smile more," Mirana leans against me. Her skin is warm.

I shrug and glance at Kaidin. He watches us now, his daughter under his arm, babbling to him.

"Things are as well as they can be," I take my eyes from his.

"Are they?" she nudges me. "It's been over a spin around the sun since…"

We don't speak of it aloud anymore.

"I know," I say.

"Wouldn't he want you to be happy?" she leans down, trying to grab my attention.

I shrug again, "I don't know if it will make me happy."

"I don't think it'll hurt," she pushes a lock of hair behind my ear. "But only if you want to, Lendhi."

I nod and she stands, going back to the stream. Our children giggle and run from her as she pretends to be a big cat sprung from the brush. Kaidin's daughter toddles after. This is a rare day he has to himself and he spends it with us. The children.

There are things about him that remind me of Ren. Funny things like mannerisms. Even how he looks from different angles. But there are many things that are different. Years ago, before the Hunt, I never dreamed I would hesitate when it came to Kai.

The Hunt.

Another will come. And another. And another. I watch my daughter crawling around. A boulder settles in my stomach. Someday she'll be a catch. Maybe. Seer, I hope not. I sigh and brush my fingers through her golden hair. She rolls over onto her back and kicks her chubby legs into the air. As my daughter giggles and laughs, I know who has the power to change the Hunt. I glance up to Kaidin, finding his gaze still on me. Maybe he can protect my daughter, or my niece.

I hate myself for thinking it, but I'll talk to him. I'll ask.

I slip from bed, Mirana's sleeping form rolls over in my absence, taking up space.

The stone floor cools my hot feat and I pad upstairs to Kai's room. I remember the layout and navigate in darkness with ease. I startle a guard walking the halls and we stare at each other. He smiles and steps aside. Heat flushes my cheeks. This isn't why I'm going up to Kaidin, but I suppose it doesn't hurt for the guard to think it. I am supposed to be his wife, after all. I slip past and open the wooden door to the room I once shared with Ren.

My heart aches, but in the dim light the room

is different. A different bed. In a different location. Different furs and decorations and colors. Thank the Seer. Perhaps Jokinah did this. Perhaps Kaidin. It doesn't matter.

I find Kaidin in bed, but like Renhin, he sleeps light. He sits up when I close the door, no matter I'm quiet, and I lean back against it. His eyes find me in the moonlight. His muscular form is naked on top of the furs. I avert my gaze as he stands, in no hurry, to pull a wrap around his waist. He pads over to me.

"Lendhi?" he whispers. "What is it?"

I bite my bottom lip as he tucks his thumb under my chin. He lifts my face and I meet his gaze.

"I'm worried," I whisper.

His brows furrow, "What about?"

I sigh, "The Hunt."

He nods and slides his arm around my shoulder, guiding me to sit in a bamboo chair cushioned with furs next to the dark fire pit. Unburned wood is piled beside it.

"I'm not taking another hutmate," he releases me.

I shake my head, "I don't want Windhi in a Hunt."

Kaidin sits in another chair across from me, "She won't be."

"She won't?" I perk up.

He shakes his head, "No. The chief's daughter doesn't have to. Neither do his sons. A chief's son can claim any woman at any time. And daughters…usually the chief decides who his daughter binds to."

"But she isn't your daughter," I point out

against my better judgement.

"She is now," he smiles. "She became mine once our ceremony was complete."

We both know it isn't complete. For the first time in ages my stomach stirs. I press my thighs together, banishing thoughts of consummation.

"You are too good to me," I mutter.

He chuckles, "Trying to make up for lost time."

"You don't owe me anything," I meet his dark blue gaze.

"Don't I?" his smile dies.

We sit in silence. I shift under his stare and stand. He remains seated, but takes hold of my hand as I pass. I look down at him and he keeps eye contact with me as he kisses my palm. My breath hitches and my heart flutters. I think I may want him.

He releases me and I offer him a smile. I go downstairs and roll my sister over so I can lay in bed. And think about Kai all night.

YEAR THREE

An attack takes us by surprise.

Midday, in the market, with a guard, I pick up food for our stores when a warning cry pierces the lull of conversation. My guard takes hold of my arm and pulls me against the nearest stall. He presses me to the ground at his feet, readjusting the grip on his spear. My protector has experience with raids and battle, but he sweats, his eyes darting every which way. I stay down and quiet. Thanking the Seer my children are safe at home.

Horns sound. Our own warriors, a new group formed from the hunters, charge through the marketplace. My guard stamps his feet, but stays close me. As does Jokinah's somewhere else. As does those who guard the house. Mirana. My children.

I watch my protector. I don't even know his name.

Our warriors chase off the enemy. Kaidin leads his men and comes back to our stone house covered in blood as the sun dips below the horizon. As his wife, taking the place of Jokinah, it is my duty and honor to wash him.

When left alone in his room, I check Kai for wounds. Making sure the blood coating his skin isn't his. My heart pounds in my throat. I can't lose Kai too. I can't handle it again. I can't—

Kaidin gently nudges me away.

"You don't have to do this," he approaches a tub full of water cloudy with herbs and soap.

I scowl and walk up, staying his hands reaching for the ties on his wrap.

"I want to," I pull the ties loose. He looks down at me. My heart thuds in my chest. I really do want to.

His hand brushes my cheek as his wrap falls and I study him. Naked.

Heat flushes my face and neck. His hand slides down to rest on my hip.

"Lendhi," his breath ghosts along the crown of my hair. "You don't have to."

"I know," my hands glide down, making trails in congealing blood, to the muscles of his lower abdomen. He sucks in air through his teeth, hissing as I circle my fingers around his length. He hardens under my grasp and heat coils between my legs.

Kaidin's hand slides up into my hair and he tilts my face up towards his. His eyes glisten with heat as they stare into mine. My lips part of their own volition. I pull away and step back. His half closed eyes widen and he clears his throat, releasing me. He steps into the tub and sinks down into the water. I kneel next to him, washing him with a sea sponge. He moans and relaxes back.

The water darkens with blood and dirt and soon he stands. I dry him from top to bottom with fur after he steps out, dripping, onto the rug. I tie a clean wrap around his waist, ignoring the proof of his desire erect between his legs.

"Goodnight," I dip down in respect.

Kaidin opens his mouth, hesitates, then, "Goodnight, Lendhi."

YEAR FOUR

This is how we live.

I fight my yearning for Kaidin. He remains impassive with subtle hints at what our relationship can be.

Back into the wet months, again into the dry. We approach the heat. My sons walk and talk on their own. Kaidin takes what little free time he has to teach them, and my nephews, how to make weapons. How to use them.

Windhi's little hand rests in mine as we watch her brothers.

Her golden brows furrow and she stands on chubby legs, with my help, "Dada!"

My heart aches. She calls for Kaidin, who rewards her with a smile. Why wouldn't she? He is the only father she knows. But still, grief washes over me. Windhi wouldn't know Ren if she saw him.

My daughter toddles out of my grasp on chubby legs to Kaidin, who holds his hands out for her. He's so good to the children. All of them. His, mine, Mirana's. I can't help but smile as he picks her up and pats her bottom. He glances at me and lifts his brows before turning back to the boys, holding her. He instructs them on how to hold their new little weapons. How the balance works. How to aim. And eventually throwing and sparring. Most of what he says I know, as he taught me in the same patient manner what feels a lifetime ago.

I draw my knees up and hug them. Mirana approaches from the stone house with two guards in tow. I watch as she passes me to speak with Kaidin. He pauses, holding Windhi, as she speaks to him in a low voice. I start when she jumps to wrap her arms around my husband. He smiles and for a brief, shameful, moment I wonder. I wonder if maybe my sister doesn't visit his bed at night. She is a woman too. She has needs. He has needs. I hate myself for this jealousy.

She releases Kaidin and jumps up into the arms of one of the guards and kisses him. My eyes widen and Kaidin glances at me. I stand and approach.

"Oh, Lendhi," Mirana releases the guard, but keeps hold of his hand. "Heitin and I are going to be hutmates."

"What?" I blink. "What?

She nods, beaming. It reaches her eyes. True happiness. I study the guard. Handsome. Older, but in good shape. He doesn't even look at me. He's too busy staring at her. How did I not notice this? How can I not see? I think of only death, and Ren, and my children, and Kaidin. Shame flushes my cheeks. Poor Mirana. I tell myself I take care of her, but I don't even notice when she falls in love. I'm selfish.

"That's wonderful," I smile. Truly, I'm happy for her. All this time I never think of Mirana having another hutmate. It's unusual, but Mirana's hutmate died. She wasn't cast off. No different than Kaidin taking me.

Mirana hugs me.

"Kaidin gave us permission," she whispers into my ear. "Thank you, Lendhi. If it wasn't for you and him this wouldn't have happened."

I can't tell her anything, because I had nothing to do with it. I hug her and offer my congratulations. Selfishly, I fear being alone. I always have Mirana. I can endure what I have to because of her. But as a new hutmate she'll have her own house to take care of. Her own children. Including new children with this man. The boys stand together with their small spears, watching with confusion. I worry they won't see each other as much. My boys will be lonely for their cousins.

And now it's inevitable my niece and nephews will be participants in the Hunt.

YEAR FIVE

During cold months I miss Mirana more than anything and invite the boys to sleep with me. They take up space she once did. They can't sleep in their pen any longer. Windhi occupies it alone, bundled in furs and close to the fire.

Flower months come and a new Hunt is underway. As chief, Kaidin oversees the ceremony with Perst in place of the elders. Their duties shrink while his grows. I stay home with the children and Jokinah and Ankhi. Jokinah speaks with me a little since Mirana left, but her and Ankhi keep to themselves.

At night I still cry for Ren. Wishing to wake up in his warm embrace and hope to Seer this is all a bad dream, but things can be worse. Always. I don't touch Kaidin since the night I bathed him, but now my thoughts linger on him in the darkness. I dream of his body over mine. Of his scent and warm hands. I wake up wanting and push those thoughts from my mind until I lay in the darkness again.

I weep for Ren while my desire for Kaidin haunts me.

It's time.

Tensions with the enemy tribe increase and Kaidin returns home later and later from meetings and plans.

I sit up for him, in his room, clean and ready, waiting for him on the bed wearing my best skins, over the layers of furs and sealskin blankets. The moon rises before sunset and a fire blooms in the hearth to combat cold rain outside. Fire makes my shadow dance on the wall as darkness sweeps over the village. I tuck my legs up under myself as my nerves tighten my muscles. I take deep breaths. The heat between my legs coils at the thought of his touch.

The wooden door opens and Kai doesn't notice me. He closes it, leaning his forehead against the wood. He shrugs off his wet cloak and it crumples at his feet. He sighs and rolls, his back against the door, his eyes closed. When he opens them, his dark blue gaze snaps to me. I flush under his stare. He freezes, leaning against the door, and I know the glaze coating his eyes too well. I never thought to see it again.

He knows what I'm here for.

I can't make myself move, frozen in place as he pushes off the door to close the distance between us. He stands over me, looking down, before his large hand cups my cheek. I close my eyes and nuzzle his palm. He crouches in front of the bed, eye level with me. I wrap my fingers around his wrist and hold his hand against me. I smooth my palm over his tense shoulders and neck. He leans in and our lips meet. Warm. Rough from wind and sun. He coaxes my mouth open and consumes me with his kiss, yanking me from the bed to crush against him.

Oh Seer, how I missed this feeling.

I circle my arms around his neck as he sits on the ground, pulling my hips to cradle his. The hardness of his desire presses against the hide separating us. His hands slide down to my hips and backside, kneading flesh. It takes my breath away and I part our kiss with a gasp. His mouth covers my face and neck as his hands find the delicate bow of my skins and pulls it loose. Heat flushes my chest as they fall and he cups my breast in his hand. He leans downward, one arm curling around me, tipping my breasts upward, and latches onto my rosy nipple. I moan and card my fingers through his thick black hair.

His muscles flex as he lifts me onto the bed, laying me back and crawling over me. I reach between us, untying the bindings of his hide wrap, and pull it away from him. He slides the hide wrapped around my hips open. He sits up, my legs sprawling around him, and I cross my arms over myself as his eyes drink me. First he stares into my eyes, then slides down, slowly, resting on the breasts I cover with my hands, and my stomach bearing the marks of a mother, and between my legs. He smiles and leans over to kiss me, the moist head of his girth sweeping over my abdomen.

I moan against his lips.

Kaidin's fiery kisses travel around my neck and down my collar bone. My fingers card into his hair as he sucks on each of my breasts, consuming their flesh with his mouth. I arch my back when his mouth hovers over the nestling of hair between my legs. He splits my moist lips before leaning in with his tongue, running it up my slit. Nerves shoot up my spine as pleasure clouds cognizant thought. I cry out, gripping the fur blankets beneath as he brings me quickly to squeeze with his tongue and fingers.

I pant, relaxing back into the soft bed, as he licks a stripe up from my bellybutton to my neck.

"Lendhi," he murmurs, his girth penetrating, as I come down from my high.

My face twists as friction distracts me from all thought. My arms circle his muscular shoulders and I hook my ankles behind him, my legs swaying with the slow rhythm he creates. His mouth meets mine and our kiss is slow and lazy. The fire burns as we sweat and pant through the night. I cry out, unashamed, without guilt, clawing my nails into his back, as he warms my insides. He moans, gripping me, crushing me to him. He stills, softening in me, and pants. He kisses me and we share our breath. I run my fingers through his thick hair and close my eyes.

"Sweet Seer," he pants against my neck.

We fall asleep, attached, and in the morning before sunrise he curls up around me, his fingers playing between my legs. I blush, recalling where I am. Who I'm with. His hand slides down to my knee and lifts my leg. He pushes into me from behind and takes me by surprise, but I moan, leaning over onto my stomach. Hot. Fast. A frenzy in comparison to last night. He presses me down as I whine into the blanket for him.

He whispers, as I squeeze around him and his seed warms my insides, "My Lendhi." He kisses the nape of my neck. "Mine."

YEAR SIX

The Hunt comes and goes. As does the rest of this spin around the sun. In the wet months I give Kaidin a son and the village celebrates with a gathering of dancing, food, festivities, and a ceremony. I gave Renhin three, but he wasn't yet chief, and this is a new celebration for all of us. Exhaustion weighs me down to the fur covered chair set out in the village center next to Kai's, which is empty. I get to hold my new baby, Sandarin, named by Kaidin, the whole time. I stare into his new eyes, a dark blue like the sea at storm. Like his father. My heart aches for Renhin, but as Kai laughs and drinks and accepts congratulations from the whole village with a gleam in his eye, I smile. I don't know if I love Kaidin as I do Ren, but I'm happy. I think he is too.

Mirana approaches with her hutmate, Heitin, and bends over to kiss my son's forehead.

"How do you feel?" she strokes his soft raven hair back from his face.

I shrug and glance down at my baby, "Same

as I have with every other. I will die for him."

She smiles, "Yes."

"But, I'm happy he'll grow up to know his father," I stroke my newborn's cheek.

"And he will be the next chief," she says.

Heitin holds her hand, smiling down at us. Mirana's own womb grows each day. She's so happy. I'm happy for her.

We both lost a hutmate, but it's not uncommon. Not with raids and animal attacks and sickness. While I did celebrate Pandin's demise, I wonder if Ren's untimely death is my fault. The Seer punishing me. Perhaps I brought Ren's death down on him by loving him and hoping for Pandin to die.

Mirana dances with her hutmate and Sandarin sleeps in my arms.

Despite music and laughter and singing, I fall asleep with my baby bundled against me in a sling.

I wake up in the night to find Kaidin missing from our bed.

Stretching, I yawn and get up, slipping on a hide wrap, as we rut almost nightly, and check on my baby. He wriggles in his sleep in the cradle fashioned from bamboo and furs. I smile and run my finger down his chubby cheek. Kaidin loves his son.

A thump seizes my attention and I pause, holding my breath, listening. A voice like a murmur in a dream drifts in from the hallway past our closed door. Another joins it. I sneak up and lean against the door to listen.

"—him."

Kaidin sighs, "Looks like you invested in the wrong son."

"Perhaps," Zerendin answers.

My heart thuds in my chest, threatening to stop. What?

"I am chief, and he is dead," I can hear the smile in Kaidin's voice. "I made sure of it."

I cover my mouth with my hand, willing myself not to cry out. Shaking, I force myself to breathe.

"What did you do?" Zerendin asks.

"I slit his throat," Kaidin whispers. "And I made damn sure to leave his body for the gulls." Barely audible. I don't catch the rest of what he says.

"Why? Why kill your own brother?" agony coats Zerendin's speech. I didn't think him capable of emotion.

Grief, and unspeakable anger, clutch my heart in a cold fist. Kaidin killed Ren? They're brothers? I don't understand.

"He took Lendhi from me," Kaidin says.

"All this over a woman?" Zerendin asks. "That woman—"

"Is my wife," Kaidin snaps. "Speak ill of her again and I'll kill you too. You can join your son in the grave."

Zerendin's voice shakes, "He has no grave. Because of you, it seems." A pause. "Your own brother. The Seer will punish you for this."

"Only because you have no power," Kaidin spits. "He was only my half-brother. As you always reminded me."

I can't listen to this anymore. I stagger back to

bed. Tears well my eyes and spill onto my cheeks. I bunch up the fur blanket and rock, holding onto it like a child. I don't understand. Kaidin doesn't know his father. Right? But…it's not impossible to think while Tannah struggled with babies Zerenden would visit Banki's hut. Sired another son. Just in case. But Kaidin, if he's Ren's half brother…Why? Why? Panic thunders around my chest and I can't breathe. I clutch my head and curl up my legs. The door opens and Kaidin shuts it, turning to me. He freezes and calculates. Trying to determine if I heard.

"Lendhi?" he moves forward, closing the distance between us.

I shake my head. His weight dips down the furs of our bed and his warm arms pull me against him.

I want to recoil. I want to slap his hands away and call him a murderer. Instead I tremble, trying to think.

"What is it?" he swallows.

I force myself to say, "I had a bad dream."

He breathes out, slow, and runs his fingers through my loose hair.

"Tell me about it," his voice rumbles against my ear.

"I dreamt you were dead," I whisper. In truth, it was a nightmare for me. Until tonight. Dread made me think Kaidin would be stolen from me like Ren was. I clench my hands into fists, forcing myself to stay in his arms.

"Oh Lendhi," he looks into my eyes, wiping my cheeks with his thumbs. "I'm not going anywhere. I will be here for you. Always."

That's what I'm afraid of. I nod, my stomach

lurching. His touch makes my heart stop and skin crawl. He killed Ren. He killed Ren. He. Killed. Ren.

I sob and cover my face with my hands.

My husband's killer comforts me as I cry. I mourn not only Ren, but Kaidin. The Kaidin I thought I knew. The Kaidin I loved. The Kaidin I now fear. If he killed Ren without a second thought, what might he do to me? My children? I have to keep it together. For them.

I have to.

Kaidin raises with the sun and is gone, as usual, when I wake.

Today I'm thankful for his absence. I lay under the warmth of the blankets, contemplating what to do. Can I do anything? Can I kill him? What would happen then? For certain my life would end. I don't mind that as much. Then I can be with Ren, but I have to think of my children.

I get up and dress before tending to my baby. I study his dark blue eyes. He needs me. I can't leave him, or my other babies, to an uncertain fate. Mirana will take them, if she can. Or they may end up in Banki's hut like the others. Carrying my newborn son in a sling, I head to the stream.

I sit on the new grass of the embankment and watch the water.

Tears blur my vision. A scream erupts from my throat and I bend over. My baby cries on my back with me. My sobs shake him. I hug myself. I rutted with Ren's killer. I loved him. I gave him a child. My betrayal drowns me. What must Ren think? The Seer?

A hand brushes my shoulder and instinctively I push it away. Arms circle around me and a voice murmurs against my ear. Soft. Sweet.

I lean into the embrace, my cheek resting over breasts. Wailing against them, rocking into their comfort, I finish my mourning cry.

Sniffing, I pull away.

Tears flow down Ankhi's cheeks. She keeps my hands in hers. Her beautiful black hair and dark eyes rival my own in coloring, but her skin is pale like the moon. Instead of a smile, her brows furrow and she cups my cheek in her delicate hand.

"What's wrong?" her voice lilts like a songbird.

My face crumples with renewed agony. I shake my head.

"I can't, tell you," I swallow. I try to pull away, but she keeps hold of me.

"Please, tell me," she whispers. "I won't say a word."

I believe her. This is the first time we speak alone. She keeps to herself. Her empathy is clear with her wet pale cheeks and glazed eyes.

Taking a deep breath, "Kaidin killed Renhin." I can't finish the sentence without crying. "I heard him say so last night."

Ankhi's mouth gapes and she pulls me against her again, careful of my son. I shudder and cry, sobbing, my baby quiet and cried out behind me. He wriggles. I straighten, but Ankhi keeps her hands on me, coaxing, comforting.

"He didn't…tell you, did he?" she dips down to catch my attention.

I shake my head, "I overheard him talking to Zerendin."

Swallowing, I frown.

"You knew," I draw from her.

She lets me go, nodding. "We both did."

We. She means Jokinah.

I press the back of my hand to my mouth, willing myself to quiet.

"I'll kill him," I whisper.

Ankhi shakes her head, taking hold of my hand.

"Don't," she squeezes. "Don't, Lendhi. It will do no good. It won't bring Renhin back."

"I must avenge him," I wipe my cheeks. "No one else will."

"You don't just condemn yourself if you kill Kai," she says. "You condemn us all. Your children. My child. Me." Ankhi sobs and my eyes snap to her, "I know it's selfish of me to ask, but you have to go on. What's done is done." She continues, "I begged him not to. I begged Jokinah to think of another way. They didn't listen to me. Oh, Lendhi, I'm so sorry."

She drops her hands and cries into them, leaning over. Her guilt washes over her in waves and my hand rests on her back.

"I told them not to," her hands muffle her voice. "I'm so sorry. I'm so sorry."

I want to cry with her, to finally have someone mourn with me, but I dry up like a well.

She's right. I must condemn myself for everyone else. Perhaps this is my true punishment from the Seer. For Pandin's death, I have to endure my husband's killer. Sleep with him. Give him pleasure. Tell him I love him. It won't be the death I hope for myself, but it will be a death all the same.

Ankhi's sobs quiet.

"Do you know what happened?" my voice breaks. "How it was done?"

She shakes her head.

"I know little," she wipes her eyes. "Only that he had to have you. From the beginning Kai and Jokinah plotted. She would get me and him you. When you went with Ren, Kai seemed all right with it. But he grew lonely. And filled with jealousy and hatred. When Yondin returned from the enemy village, a deal of some kind was made. The battle? It wasn't really a battle. Only those loyal to Ren died in that fight with him. Every raid, every fight since, only Kaidin's enemies parish. We aren't truly at war with the other tribe. Arde was returned to his father years ago."

I cover my mouth with my hand, eyes widening.

"I knew he would come for you," she continues. "He has to have you, Lendhi. He won't let you go. He'll do anything to keep you."

Including kill for me.

I shake my head. This isn't love. This is something else. An unnamed thing lurking within the darkness of the underworld. A place where the Seer's light doesn't shine. Where His eyes cannot see.

I put it off for as long as I can, but when I can't wait any longer it's torture to lay with Kaidin. I do as I must. At first I think it impossible to be convincing, but each time it gets easier. Each time I know what sounds to make, what things to do, to make him think he pleases me.

Fear grips me in the night. When sweat covers our bodies and I lay in his arms. My feet itch to run. To grab my children and be free of him, but it's impossible. He's the chief now. While I can take my children from Zerendin, taking them from Kaidin is a different matter. And where will I take them? Back to Ren's hut to live in filth and hunger? No. I have to stay. I must.

I'm so alone.

When Erdin tells me I catch another child, tears spring into my eyes.

Tannah furrows her brows, putting her arm around my shoulders, "Lendhi?"

I shake my head. Erdin excuses herself from the small room of the healing hut. I lean against Tannah.

"Lendhi, what's wrong? Kaidin will be so happy."

"I know," I sniff, wiping my hands over my wet face. "He will be."

"Why the tears?"

I shake my head again. I can't tell her.

Leaving the healer hut, I part ways with

Tannah and order my guard to leave me be. He's reluctant, but I'm firm and assure him I'm fine. Instead of returning home, I search for Mirana.

She's alone, her baby slung to her back while she gathers fresh water from the stream into water skins. She hums and kneels on the soft embankment. Sunlight shines down on her past the canopy of trees.

She glances up when I kneel next to her.

"Len?" her brows furrow. "What's wrong?"

My breath shudders. I crumble and sob as her warm arm comes round my shoulders. I lean into her and she rubs my back.

"Seer, what is it?" her face grows close to mine.

I shake my head and she remains silent as I cry. Sniffling, I take a shuddering breath.

"Child," I shake.

He brows furrow, "You're not happy?"

"No," I cover my face.

"Why? Kaidin will be plea—"

"He killed Ren!" I clutch my head and pull from her. "I don't care what pleases him."

Mirana's mouth hangs agape and she searches the brush around us. She leans in and whispers, "What? He killed him?"

I nod, keeping my hands over my face.

"Oh, Seer," she pulls me to her. "Oh Len, how do you know?"

I wipe my eyes and stare down at the bubbling water in front of us.

"I overheard it. He told Zerendin…and he's…he's Ren's half brother. He killed him for me. Me," I drag out the last word in agony. My worst fear is true. I caused Ren's death. "I don't want to have this baby."

Tears spring into my sister's eyes. They fall down her cheeks and she holds me close.

"You're sure?" she asks.

"Yes," I clear my throat. "Ankhi...she told me the truth."

"How long have you known?" she asks.

"Long enough."

"That..." she swallows. "Len, I have to tell you something."

My heart seizes. Dread coats her voice.

"Heitin told me something and I debated telling you but," she bites her lip. A trait we share. "Maybe I should."

Curiosity anchors my emotion and I wipe my eyes, enjoying her warmth and comfort.

"Go on," I sniff.

"Kaidin ordered him to take me as a hutmate."

I cock my brow and scowl, "He was trying to get rid of you? But, you're so happy an—"

"I am happy. I am. Heitin and I do care for each other. Really. He was interested in me before that, and Kaidin jumped on the opportunity, but it bothers Heitin now. He didn't think much of it at first, but he finally told me. He doesn't want secrets between us."

She hesitates. Her eyes dart around us, searching for spies. She lowers her voice, "Kaidin asked me to...gently nudge you into his embrace too."

I gasp.

"He was so convincing," she speaks quickly. "In his love for you and I just want you to be happy, but now…hearing this…I don't know what to make of it. This isn't healthy. Whatever this is. It doesn't seem like real love to me."

I nod, wondering what else Kaidin does I don't know about.

"I want to leave," I look down.

Mirana takes hold of my shoulders and turns me to face her.

"You can't. Think of your children. Renhin has left them in your care. You must stay. You must," she wipes my wet cheeks. "I know it's hard. I really do know, but you can't let them go hungry. You can't let them suffer. The suffering is yours to bear, not theirs."

She sounds like Ankhi, but she's right. As Ankhi is. I made the decision to put them first when I carried and named them.

"I will stay," I sigh.

"Len," Kaidin calls to me like the chief and not my husband as I approach the stone house.

His brows furrow. I hesitate and stop, sensing his anger. It rolls off of him like waves of heat in the warm months.

"Where did you go?" his hands cup my upper arms. "Without a guard? Erdin told me you caught another child and cried. What's wrong? What's going on? Do you have any idea how worried I've been?"

I frown. Erdin's betrayal will be dealt with later. Maybe. If I have the energy.

"I went to tell Mirana the big news," I allude.

He can assume what big news all he wants. "I'm tired. That's all. I'm tired from babies." This is true. His face softens and he pulls me against him, tucking my hair back behind my ears.

"Of course," he strokes my hair and rests his chin atop my head. "After this one we can see Erdin about it."

I nod and snake my arms around his middle, fingers splaying over his bare muscular back, fantasizing about running a bone knife through it.

"You have more important things to worry about," I try to pull away, but he holds me to him. "I'm fine."

"I would do anything for you," he kisses the crown of my head. "Anything."

My heart seizes up. I know he's truthful about this, at least.

YEAR SEVEN

I birth my sixth child, Galadin, another son for Kaidin.

I refuse Erdin anymore business. Banki gives me the herbs I need to avoid catching another child. The old woman helped care for Mirana and I when our parents died. She did Kaidin too, but I try not to think of him. I take the herbs with water in the morning. Weeks pass. Then months.

I can't take my hatred for his father out on him, so I love my baby with all my heart. His older siblings love him and play with him. His cousins. It's not his fault. I regret not wanting him, but he's here now and I will do anything for him.

Kaidin presses me down onto my back, penetrating my body with his girth, and spills his seed into me. He pants, sagging over me. I lay back, panting, my forearm thrown over my eyes. Tonight is difficult. I did my best, and it seems to be enough. My forearm slides down and Kai kisses my forehead and pushes my hair back from my face. He kisses my lips.

I feign sleep, as I often do after we rut. I don't want to snuggle. I don't want to talk to him. I use the care of the children as an excuse and he accepts it. Soon, with his arm draped over me, his breath evens out and I'm left alone with my thoughts in the moonlight.

Bugs chirp from the brush. The guards speak in low tones outside the stone house. Everyone is at peace. Everyone, but me.

I hate him. I. Hate. Him.

My heart races when my eyes settle over his bone knife resting on his skins by the bed. Similar to Ren's. Perhaps the same knife he used to slit my love's throat.

I slip from Kai's grasp and he rolls onto his stomach, his hand reaching for me. I pause, watching his eyes flutter back into the dream land. Swallowing, and naked, I kneel by the pile of Kaidin's wrap and weapons. I grab the knife and slip it from the hide sheath. Running my finger along the sharp edge, I suck in my breath when it breaks the skin of my index finger.

If I am what Kaidin loves most, perhaps I can ensure a future for my children and still be free of this pain.

I contemplate. I want to be with Renhin. I want to be in his arms again. To tell him I love him. To hear him say my name. Tears spill down my cheeks as I bring the point of the knife to my stomach.

A strong hand grips mine and I cry out as Kaidin wrestles with me. I turn and try to bring the blade down on him. In the darkness he overpowers me. It's no contest. I lose the knife and cry as he keeps my wrists in a bruising grip. He pants and crushes me to him. I cry into his chest.

"I hate you," I strain against him. "I hate you."

His breath increases and though I struggle, he keeps me still against him.

"So you know," his voice rumbles in my ear.

I can only sob.

"Lendhi," his hand smooths down my hair. "I had to. You don't understand. I had to."

I can't tell if he's trying to convince me, or himself.

"I had to do it," he whispers.

"I will kill myself," my voice is hoarse. "And be rid of you."

"No," he pulls me away, holding my face in his hands. "You won't."

"I will," I muster conviction. "I will."

His eyes narrow, "If you do, your sons will join you soon after. And your daughter."

I gasp, my breath short.

"I don't want them to be separated from their mother," he dares to lean in and kiss my forehead. "Like we were from ours."

I tremble in his embrace.

"Do you understand?" his thumb rubs my cheek.

"You wouldn't," I choke. "You wouldn't."

"Wouldn't I? I will, my beautiful Lendhi," he

leans in, his lips ghosting against mine. We share breath as I take shuddering gasps. "I. Will."

"All right," my face crumples. I let him kiss me. "All right. I'll stay."

I'm sorry, Ren.

With the passage of time my horror remains, but I control it. Leash it. I bend my body to his will and he continues as though nothing has happened. He continues as though I don't know he murdered the love of my life. As though he doesn't threaten my children.

Eventually, I can make myself continue as well.

But I always see blood on his hands. Hear jealousy in his voice. Feel possession in his touch.

The village thrives under his watch. The enemy tribe keeps their distance and Ankhi's confession of his connection with them makes more sense as time goes by. Kaidin never worries. Never waivers. He knows we'll all be fine. Our village. Our children. Our bond.

I wish I had his confidence. His knowledge of the future.

YEAR ELEVEN

My boys, Ren's boys, celebrate their tenth spin around the sun. In the stone house we serve fruit carved into flowers, and meats smoke over a large spit set up for the occasion. Kaidin gives them new spears he made himself and a gift of sealskins. Soon they will hunt with him properly. My heart swells each time I look at them. They look so much like their father. Ren in triplicate. Only Vandin, the youngest triplet, looks anything like me, but it's his hair alone. He has his father's eyes and height and nose and mouth and—

Windhi squeals as Kaidin picks her and his own daughter up to twirl in his arms. The boys dance around him out in the courtyard. Including my two youngest, Kaidin's sons. His threats on their lives a distant memory. How he is with them, I wonder at the truth of it. At times like this, when my children smile as bright as their future, I'm thankful he kept me here. But not thankful he used them as a road to do so.

I glance down a moment to the fruit I carve and when I look back up, Kai's eyes rest on me. Always, his eyes are on me. I shift under his gaze and pass out bits of fruit to visiting children. My boys' friends. Some prominent village members, and others invited to this celebration. Ankhi works next to me. We don't speak ever again as we did that day years ago. She smiles as she watches the children at play.

I wear a smile out of habit. Perhaps she does as well.

The children squeal and play with the chief before running up to consume sweet fruit Jokinah's family gave to us for the occasion. Her parents attend with my sister and her family. Zerendin and Tannah show. Surrounded by people, some who love me, some who don't, I feel isolation. My heart thuds slow. I'm half dead. Knowing I lay with my husband's killer nightly. Knowing I bore him two sons. My baby, Galadin, runs up to hug my leg and I can't help a smile.

Kaidin is a good father. A good husband. I try not to think of what a brother he was. To this day I don't tell anyone else. After the night with Kaidin, where he found a way to hold me to him always, I don't speak of it again. I can only smile at my children, pretend for my murderous husband, and hope someday soon I can join Ren in death.

Moonlight shines into our room as Kaidin lays me on my back to push into me.

I moan and react how he likes. How I might

have done when I loved him. I curl my legs around his hips as his girth glides in and out of my body. I amaze and shame myself. How I can will my body to do as he pleases. It isn't as difficult as it once was. He remains hard and lean, muscular. I can pretend he's someone else for at least a rut.

Wind blows in from the balcony, pushing away lingering heat of day as we lay on our shared bed. Kaidin kisses around my face and neck, gripping my knees at his sides to widen my legs. I whimper and his hot mouth consumes mine.

"I want another son," he whispers against my lips. "Give me another son. I want to watch you grow big with my seed again."

He asks this every night lately.

I pretend his touch consumes me and reply with a gasp and moan.

Violently he jerks up, out of, and away from me.

A masked warrior ties Kai's arms behind his back while two others hold him still. A buzz fills the air as something made of black shiny stone attaches to Kai's stomach. Lightening shoots out of the small thing in our attacker's hand. Kai cries out, his muscles bunching. The buzzing stops and so does the small lightening. Kai hangs limp before fighting back, but he's no match for them. Or for the small weapon sending lightening through him in short bursts. He lays limp in their grasp, panting, and they drag him from the room.

I scramble for a fur blanket to cover my naked skin. My breath can't come fast enough. My heart hammers in my throat and chest and head and tears spring into my eyes.

I don't recognize this tribe. Their paint and masks are new colors. Their weapons and skins different. Instead of bone, their spearheads have the shiny bone of the ancients, reflective and grey, like the piece Perst keeps in her chest. Instead of hide wraps and loincloths, their clothing covers their legs and torso. Things over their feet. Each of them wears a mask, like an animal. A big cat, a seal, a deer, and more.

They surround the bed as Kaidin shouts threats from the hallway. He screams out from beneath the gag they stuff into his mouth.

The warriors turn back to me and one stands out from the others. The one in the deer mask. His intense eyes penetrate mine from behind the mask. His light gaze causes a flush to coat my neck and chest in the moonlight.

My children scream.

I launch from the bed and mow down one of the assailants. He grunts behind his seal mask as my fist strikes into his neck. He gasps and coughs as others pull me from him. The warrior in the deer mask takes time to cover my shoulders with a cloak and tie it before wrapping his arms around me to lift me away. He holds me calm and close, his warm breath puffing out from beneath the mask and into my hair. Tears well my eyes. Kaidin is gone. They drag the children into the room, including Jokinah's daughter and the deer man holding me faces me to the small line up.

My boys, bound, fight and kick. Windhi cries, holding the hands of her little brothers, Kaidin's sons. My sons. Jokinah's daughter cries with her arm around Windhi.

"Lendhi," one of the men's muffled voice calls from beneath the mask of a big cat.

I freeze in my captor's grasp.

"The Seer sent us," big cat gestures to the sky.

I don't realize I hold my breath until I gasp for air.

"Which of these babes are yours?" big cat points to the line of children.

It steals my breath when the deer man holding me points to my triplets. The warriors nod and my boys scream, thrash, and fight as they're drug from the room. I wriggle, but deer holds me fast.

"Any others?" big cat asks. "There is at least one more."

"Mama," Windhi cries, tears falling down her cheeks. "Mama?"

If the Seer truly sent them, I should take Jokinah's daughter with me. We must go to a good place, but I can't separate a mother from her child. Even if it's to bring her to the Seer.

I lick my lips, "All but the little girl on the end."

They separate her from the rest and she screams, crying, as they drag her away. My face crumples as I watch. I can't do anything. For the first time in years I wish for Kai. He is bad, but a bad I know.

But do I dare question the Seer's will? Again?

The man by the children kneels and my boys hold onto Windhi's hand.

The deer presses a square of thin, soft hide against my face. A sweet smell waters my eyes as I struggle to breathe through it. Darkness surrounds my vision moments before I lose consciousness.

Pain splits my head as I come to.

Blinking my heavy eye lids, I try to sit up. A hand presses down on my shoulder. The warrior from before. The deer who held me as my children were taken away. I won't forget those eyes.

I lay back, resting my forearm over my eyes. We rock, swaying on the tide, in a longboat humming like an animal from the back end. Past my arm morning sun greys the sky. Gulls screech in the distance. The deer, who sits over me as I lay on the floor, presses another hide against my face.

Bright sunlight warms my face and I moan, rolling over to burrow into darkness.

I regain awareness, my head throbbing. Memories of last night flood my vision and I sit up, gasping, clutching my head, blinking against the piercing light. My heart pulsates in my temples, but as I press against them, the pain recedes to a dull ache.

I sit in a bed, covered in impossibly soft and fragile hide, but it isn't quite like hide. I don't know what it is. Textured. Thin. White. No animal has this kind of skin. The sea lies beyond a balcony, past a white sand beach. Warm and pleasant. Bombardment of an aroma, fruit and flowers, assaults my nostrils. I sneeze in the fresh sea air.

An intake of breath alerts me to a presence, a someone, behind me. I freeze, taking note that I now wear the same strange hides as the blanket. Heat rises to my cheeks. I was naked when they took me. I will myself to turn and face my captor.

Holy Seer.

"Ren," I whisper.

My dead husband smiles at me and it reaches his startling blue eyes. He sits on a stool in front of the bed, leaning his elbows on his knees. His golden skin is the same, his blonde hair, his muscular torso. He has only a few wrinkles around his eyes and a jagged angry scar across his neck faded with age.

"Ren," I cover my mouth with my hand. "Am I dead?"

He stands from the stool to cross over onto the bed. I leap into his warm arms. He holds me tight. Crushing me to him. Seer, he smells good. He feels so good. I can't help but cry into his bare chest. He kisses the crown of my head and he trembles, his chest heaving.

"Len," he whispers into my hair. "You're not dead. We're alive. So very much alive."

He cries with me, fluttering kisses all over my face and I smile, laughing, doing the same to him. He's real. He's alive. My Ren.

"How?" my fingers trace the features of his handsome face over and over. I don't want to ever forget it.

"Long story," he takes hold of my hand to kiss the knuckles. "But you're safe. The children are safe. We're together. All of us. And nothing, no one, will take you away from me again."

"The children. Ren, were you there? Was that you? The deer?"

He nods, running his hands over my arms.

We can't stop touching each other.

"I was. I held you while we sorted out the children. I know you didn't want to leave them there. I didn't want to either. I didn't want to alarm you. Anymore than necessary. And," his lips quirk. "I didn't want to weep in front of the others."

I laugh and he pulls me against him for a languorous kiss.

YEAR TWELVE

Ren introduces me to this new world slowly.

With care. We have a fresh start on this island. They call it the Unen. They have metal; the name of the bone left by the ancients. Other technologies too. Books. Textile. Farmland. Things to improve our lives and things to cause detriment to enemies. Or other nations.

When Ren lay dying in the sun, these people rescued him with medicine. And what they call doctors. At night, lights glow from glass. And now I understand the true history of our people.

The old ones, who walked beyond death, have a different name. Nzambi. They drove our people from the biggest of islands into the sea. Our tribes and villages on the chain of islands, numbering in the hundreds varying in size, all descended from those who survived and came over in the big metal whale. Ren says they call it a vessel. The remains of the whale lie at the bottom of the reef by the great Unen city, Dilmun. You can dive down and touch the rusted metal if you wish.

Since I woke to find Ren alive and well, our children get to know him all over again. He meets Windhi, and my boys with Kaidin, for the first time. The triplets, to my delight, have vague memories of him. His eyes are what they recall. Kaidin's sons are still young and trust easily. Every time I look at them I think of their father and the horrors he brought on my life when at one time I thought him a savior.

At times I watch the waves from our room and wonder what he's doing. He escaped from Ren and his friends the night they took me. An operation, as they call it, took some time to plan. They weren't sent by the Seer, though I argue they were without their knowing. Ren knew it was what they needed to say for my cooperation. He knew Kaidin took me and he knew I would have other children. He couldn't bare to tear me away from them. Even Kaidin's children.

Kaidin lives and sometimes in the night I wake, with a nightmare, and have to reassure myself Ren is alive and well next to me. When I drink water from a pipe in our wall and bathe in warm water at will, I think of the stream by the village. I wonder if Mirana gathers water to lug back to her hut at this moment. I fantasize telling Tannah her son is alive and well.

Sometimes I fear waking to Kaidin dragging me from our home. I clutch Ren as he comforts me and tells me it's impossible. Kaidin cannot get me. Cannot get us. But I will always look over my shoulder.

Sunset on the horizon flashes over the orange ocean waves.

Ren and I sit together, our hands entwining, always, and watch the children play in the sand.

I ask him how it came to be. Why he took so long to come get me. He tells me everything. And now I know what he went through to bring us together, but I also sometimes wonder if it isn't the Seer's own doing. They lied when they told me the Seer sent them for me, but I can't help wondering if the Seer really did aid Ren and his new companions. To bring us together. If my prayers were heard—and answered.

"Whoever did it, we're together, and that's what matters," he says, raising my hand to his lips and kissing my knuckles.

I smile.

He's right.

Ren came back from the dead for me. Kaidin lingers out there. Planning. Angry. Hunting for me, always.

I can only pray to the great Seer who brought my husband back from the dead, Kaidin doesn't find us.

Ren squeezes my hand and smiles. I sigh, returning my attention to the children who play on the beach.

The Hunt

The Hunt

ABOUT THE AUTHOR

L.R. is from Lubbock, Texas, but lives in Washington among the trees and mountains, enjoying hiking, camping, and writing when the mood suits.

Which is often.

The Hunt

More from LeeLoo Publishing!

Samiyah by L.R. Hicks

Samiyah is the ideal human woman. She lives on the ranch, the best place to buy human stock in the galaxy cluster. For years she trains to be the best sex slave money can buy. Now, the time has come for her to leave with her new master.

She begs her friend, the old Parishioner, to help her escape. When he does, her expectations disappear with the only life she has ever known.

Adventure, ancient relics, and love of different spectrums await her.

The Hunt

Dragon Bloode: Covet by Mishka Williams

Once a mighty race of winged gods, they're reduced to three. No longer do they resemble the scaled flying marvels of their ancestry, but the humans who interbred with their forefathers. The Bloode is thin and dying.

Mishka Williams's dark fantasy debut is nothing short of spellbinding. Dive into a realm rich with magic, Dragons, and lust. Set against a gothic backdrop in the world of Alperin, Williams takes you to the Draak Empire. Rife with division between the Emperor and his Dragon generals, the empire faces enemies on all fronts. From the Fae, the Elves, and from within.

The Hunt

Edge of Ridiculous by Anne Coffer

She's human. He's not.

For the most part. We're pretty sure.

Maybe a little human…humanoid at least.

George isn't her real name. Bob isn't his. When fate intervenes on the loop in Lubbock, Texas, nothing will be the same for George again. Her fantasies of a fairy tale adventure come true.

Except for the part with monsters. And the jail time. And the absolute vomit-inducing terror of creating an online dating profile.

The Hunt

Brick Wilson: Clueless by Marq Truong

Return to the Ultimate Galactic Universe with Brick Wilson as he attempts to rescue Hilep, the wealthiest man in the Ultimate Universe, who has kidnapped himself. See what happens when you surgically remove your split personality? With a crime that has even the UGH Tax Authority rendered apathetic, can Brick save the bazillionaire from his own clutches and restore illogical order to the universe?

The Hunt

If you enjoyed this, or any other title by small publishers, please leave a rating or review!

Thank you!

The Hunt